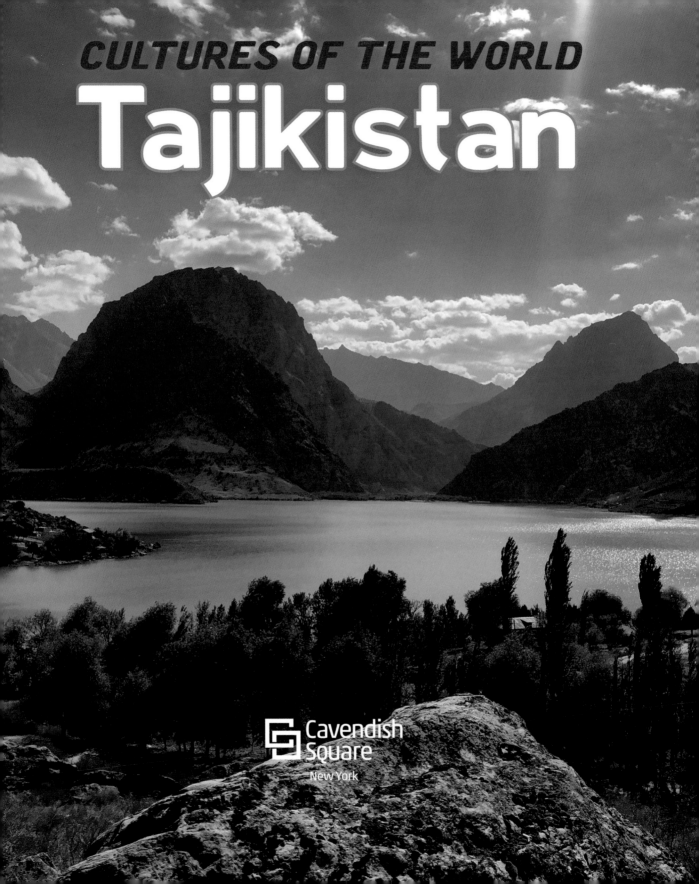

# CULTURES OF THE WORLD
# Tajikistan

Cavendish
Square
New York

Published in 2021 by Cavendish Square Publishing, LLC
243 5th Avenue, Suite 136, New York, NY 10016
Copyright © 2021 by Cavendish Square Publishing, LLC

Third Edition

Website: cavendishsq.com

This publication represents the opinions and views of the author based on his or her personal experience, knowledge, and research. The information in this book serves as a general guide only. The author and publisher have used their best efforts in preparing this book and disclaim liability rising directly or indirectly from the use and application of this book.

All websites were available and accurate when this book was sent to press.

Cataloging-in-Publication Data

Names: Abazov, Rafis. | Nevins, Debbie.
Title: Tajikistan / Rafis Abazov and Debbie Nevins.
Description: New York : Cavendish Square, 2021. | Series: Cultures of the world
Identifiers: ISBN 9781502658746 (library bound) | ISBN 9781502658753 (ebook)
Subjects: LCSH: Tajikistan--Juvenile literature. | Tajikistan--Description and travel. | Tajikistan--History--Juvenile literature. | Tajikistan--Social life and customs.
Classification: LCC DK923.A22 2021 | DDC 958.6--dc23

Writers, third edition: Rafis Abazov, Debbie Nevins
Editor, third edition: Debbie Nevins
Designer, third edition: Jessica Nevins
Picture Researcher, third edition: Jessica Nevins

**PICTURE CREDITS**

The photographs in this book are used with the permission of: Cover Nickolai Repnitskii/Shutterstock.com; p. 1 Nargis Sakhibova/EyeEm/Getty Images; pp. 3, 17, 62 Bjorn Holland/The Image Bank/Getty Images Plus; pp. 5, 34, 48, 67, 70, 108 Martin Moos/Lonely Planet Images/Getty Images Plus; p. 7 Laurie Noble/Stone/Getty Images; p. 8 Evgenii Zotov/Moment/Getty Images; p. 10 kosmozoo/DigitalVision Vectors/Getty Images; p. 13 Jaap Hooijkaas/Moment/Getty Images; pp. 14, 39 Arterra/Universal Images Group via Getty Images; p. 16 Andyworks/E+/Getty Images; p. 18 Leonid Andronov/iStock/Getty Images Plus; pp. 19, 105 cescassawin/Moment/Getty Images Plus; p. 21 Arterra/Contributor898373816/Universal Images Group Editorial/Getty Images; p. 22 PHAS/Universal Images Group via Getty Images; p. 25 Vodjani/ullstein bild via Getty Images; p. 27 mtcurado/iStock/Getty Images Plus; p. 28 Brad Gooch/Bloomberg via Getty Images; p. 31 Universal History Archive/Universal Images Group via Getty Images; p. 33 TASS via Getty Images; p. 35 Mikhail Svetlov/Getty Images; p. 36 Marcin Skowronski/iStock/Getty Images Plus; p. 40 Tajikistan Presidency Press Office/Anadolu Agency/Getty Images; p. 42 NOZIM KALANDAROV/AFP via Getty Images; p. 44 johan10/iStock/Getty Images Plus; pp. 49, 77, 80, 103, 112, 118, 126, 127, 128 Nozim Kalandarov/TASS via Getty Images; p. 52 Dieter Hopf/Getty Images; p. 55 Nevada Wier/Corbis Documentary/Getty Images Plus; p. 56 Gfed/iStock/Getty Images Plus; p. 58 Lukas Bischoff/iStock/Getty Images Plus; p. 60 Knighterrant/E+/Getty Images; pp. 69, 114 Amos Chapple/Lonely Planet Images/Getty Images Plus; pp. 73, 74 Yegor Aleyev/TASS via Getty Images; p. 84 Danita Delimont/Gallo Images/Getty Images Plus; p. 90 LUKASZ-NOWAK1/iStock Editorial/Getty Images Plus; p. 93 Bernd von Jutrczenka/picture alliance via Getty Images; p. 97 mtcurado/iStock Unreleased/Getty Images; p. 98 Frizi/iStock Editorial/Getty Images Plus; p. 101 Evgenii Zotov/Moment/Getty Images; p. 104 Ozbalci/iStock Editorial/Getty Images Plus; p. 106 Seref Ozen/iStock/Getty Images Plus; p. 111 Bradley Mayhew/Lonely Planet Images/Getty Images Plus; p. 116 Tajikistan Presidency/Anadolu Agency/Getty Images; p. 122 Nomad1988/Shutterstock.com; p. 124 Ron Ramtang/Shutterstock.com; p. 125 AlexelA/Shutterstock.com; p. 130 r401@yandex.ru/Shutterstock.com; p. 131 Fanfo/Shutterstock.com.

Some of the images in this book illustrate individuals who are models. The depictions do not imply actual situations or events.

CPSIA compliance information: Batch #CW21CSQ: For further information contact Cavendish Square Publishing LLC, New York, New York, at 1-877-980-4450.

Printed in the United States of America

Find us on

# CONTENTS

# TAJIKISTAN TODAY

**F**AR FROM ANY SHORE, DEEP IN ONE OF THE MOST FORMIDABLE mountain regions of the Eurasian landmass, the country of Tajikistan can seem— from a Western point of view—almost hidden. It's one of the five "'Stans" that make up Central Asia, the vast expanse that lies east of Europe, between China, Russia, and India. *Stan* is a Persian word that means "land of," and Kazakhstan, Kyrgyzstan, Tajikistan, Turkmenistan, and Uzbekistan are named for the ethnic peoples who live in them. (There are other "'Stans," some more familiar to Western consciousness—including Afghanistan and Pakistan—but strictly speaking, they are outside of Central Asia.)

Central Asia is a meeting point of Turkic, Persian, and Mongol cultures. This is reflected in the languages and the physical appearances of the people. Historians and archaeologists trace this region's roots to early civilizations going back about 3,000 years and claim that the early Tajik people contributed greatly to the Persian and Turkish empires. These people were famous for their fine handicrafts, and they serviced many trade caravans on the Silk Road that connected the East and West. Tajik writers produced fine poems and songs that became part of the classic literature of the

Middle East and South Asia. Tajikistan is also known for its beautiful landscapes and is home to the world's third-highest mountain system, the Pamirs.

Tajikistan, along with all the Central Asian states, also reflects the great Russian influence of its more recent domination by its massive neighbor to the north. In the late 19th century, the czarist Russian Empire expanded southward, taking what territories it wanted. In the early 20th century, that empire was violently replaced by another, the communist Soviet Union. Central Asia was forged into Soviet states. The Tajiks were forced to radically change their lifestyles. Soviet dictator Joseph Stalin drew new, somewhat arbitrary boundaries for administrative purposes. They corresponded neither to natural geographic features nor to the ethnic identities of the people living within them. Many Tajiks found themselves living in Afghanistan. Many Uzbeks were now a part of Tajikistan.

Tajikistan existed for around 70 years as a Soviet republic. It became in many ways an extension of Russia. The Tajik people learned to speak Russian, adopted Russian traditions, and learned to rely on the Communist central government in Moscow. All that fell apart as the Soviet Union finally collapsed, and Tajikistan emerged from the ashes as an independent entity in 1991.

Since that time, the Tajikistanis have struggled to keep their country united and to integrate it into the global economy. First, however, the country had to endure a bloody civil war from 1992 to 1997. The conflict began when various regional and religious groups did not agree with the newly formed government, which was dominated by people from the Khujand and Kulob regions. Anywhere from 20,000 to 100,000 people were killed in the hostilities, and 10 to 20 percent of the population was displaced. In 1992, the nation's president, Rahmon Nabiyev, was ambushed by opposition forces and compelled to resign. He died soon afterward under mysterious circumstances, and Emomali Rahmon came to power. He remains in power to this day.

Tajikistan emerged from this war as the poorest of all the former Soviet republics. Since that time, the government has made some progress in fighting poverty, lowering the poverty rate from 66.8 percent in 2003 to 29 percent in 2017. This impressive improvement reflects well on the country's leadership, but at the same time, there are increasing concerns about the long tenure of President Rahmon.

Rahmon's regime has become more and more authoritarian as political opposition is harshly stomped out, and elections are viewed as fraudulent. He has created a new post for himself as "Leader of the Nation," which frees him from constitutional term limits. In addition, he appears to be cementing his family's hold on the nation by paving the way for his son to succeed him.

Rahmon is criticized by some observers for spending billions on excessive building projects in the capital of Dushanbe. In 2010, the nation marked its 20th anniversary with what was hailed as the world's tallest flagpole. The 541-foot (165 meter) flagpole, crowned with a 98-foot by 197-foot (30 m by 60 m) national flag, can be seen from nearly all parts of Dushanbe. The flagpole's claim as the world's tallest was soon surpassed by one in Saudi Arabia, but the pole remains indicative of what some see as Rahmon's excessive "spending spree" on grand new buildings and projects that the nation cannot afford. The largest of those projects is the construction of the Rogun Dam on the Vakhsh River, which is slated to be the world's highest hydroelectric dam. This project allegedly threatens the water supply of neighboring Uzbekistan, which objects to its construction.

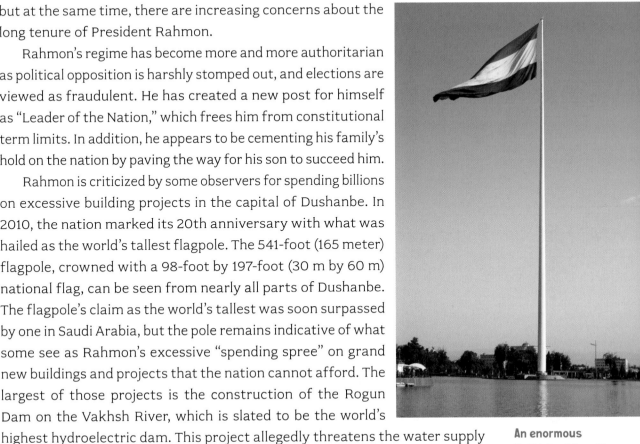

An enormous Tajikistani flag flies from the world's second-highest flagpole, which is in Dushanbe.

In the winter and spring of 2020, as the global COVID-19 pandemic was spreading rapidly across the globe, Tajikistan at first denied the presence of the illness within its borders. In March, the great public celebration of Nowruz went forward with no restrictions, and President Rahmon took part in large public gatherings. By May of that year, however, the virus was confirmed in all regions of the country, and mandatory face mask rules were put into effect. Since then, however, reliable figures relating to the pandemic have not been forthcoming, and reporters have complained of a virtual media blackout on the topic. The pandemic will certainly have a negative effect on Tajikistan's already struggling economy, as it will worldwide. At this writing, the impact remains to be seen.

# GEOGRAPHY

A green valley is surrounded by the Fann Mountains, part of the Pamir range, in Tajikistan's Sughd Province.

THE REPUBLIC OF TAJIKISTAN IS A landlocked, mountainous country in Central Asia. It has a land area of 55,637 square miles (144,100 square kilometers), making it approximately the size of the U.S. state of Iowa.

It's one of the five nations that make up Central Asia, the vast expanse of terrain that lies east of Europe and west of China. Tajikistan, like its neighbors Kazakhstan, Kyrgyzstan, Turkmenistan, and Uzbekistan, is named for the ethnic group who forms the majority of the population (in this case, the Tajiks). Of the five Central Asian nations, Tajikistan is the smallest in terms of area but lies at the highest elevation. It is more mountainous and has higher mountains than any of the others.

Tajikistan stretches for about 218 miles (351 km) from north to south and about 435 miles (700 km) from east to west. It shares borders with Afghanistan in the south, China in the east, Kyrgyzstan in the northeast, and Uzbekistan in the northwest and west.

The land that makes up present-day Tajikistan was part of various ancient Central Asian states, including the empires founded by Alexander the Great, the Persians, the Mongol warriors, and Timur (also known as Tamerlane), the Turco-Mongol conqueror who dominated western Asia in the 14th century. Tajikistan occupies the western slopes of the Pamir Mountains and the southern part of the fertile Fergana Valley. The rivers that begin in the glaciers of Tajikistan are important sources of water for drinking and irrigation not only in Tajikistan but also in neighboring Uzbekistan and Afghanistan.

## GEOGRAPHIC AND ADMINISTRATIVE REGIONS

Most of Tajikistan's fertile valleys are situated between the upper basins of two of Central Asia's major rivers: the Amu Darya and the Syr Darya. The topography of the country is characterized by alternating small fertile valleys and mountain ranges that gradually gain altitude in the east. These mountains are home to the largest glaciers in Central Asia and are the sources of many rivers.

Tajikistan's lowest point is where the Syr Darya runs through the Fergana Valley in the north. The nation's highest point—Qullai Ismoil Somoni (Ismail Somoni Peak, formerly Communism Peak during Soviet times), which is 24,590 feet (7,495 m) high—is located in the east, close to the border with Kyrgyzstan.

Tajikistan has four major regions that are quite distinct in terms of the landscape, climate, and soil found there. They correspond to the country's administrative divisions: the provinces of Sughd and Khatlon; the Region of Republican Subordination (RRP), which is also known as the Districts of Republican Subordination; and the autonomous province of Gorno-Badakhshan (GBAO).

**THE NORTHERN REGION**    This is the province of Sughd, with the provincial capital of Khujand (also spelled Khudzhand). Northern Tajikistan straddles the Zeravshan River basin and the southern Fergana Valley, which contains

*This map of Tajikistan shows its capital, Dushanbe, the nation's four major regions, and its borders with surrounding countries. It was made when the city of Bokhtar was still known as Qurghonteppa.*

some of the most fertile land in Central Asia. This is a moderately elevated area with few hills and few mountain ranges. The large, flat swaths of land are divided by rows of poplars and mulberry trees into small, well-cultivated plots. Completing the landscape are numerous human-made canals, which supply irrigation water from the Syr Darya, Zeravshan, and other rivers to the local cotton fields and apricot and apple orchards.

This is one of the most densely populated areas of the country, and thousands of villages (*kishlaks*) line the major roads. Most of the houses are built of mud bricks and painted in light colors. They usually have small gardens attached to them. This area is also home to large communities of ethnic Uzbeks.

Towns and cities have existed in this area for centuries, but few of the region's historic monuments or buildings have survived until the present day. In fact, the city of Khujand, the second-largest in the nation and one of the oldest in Tajikistan, looks quite modern. Its red-brick and concrete houses, public buildings, and factories suggest a small town in Eastern Europe, while the bazaars, or marketplaces, and several newly renovated and newly built mosques show more of a Turkish or Middle Eastern influence.

**THE CENTRAL REGION**   This is the Region of Republican Subordination. With its relatively higher mountains and numerous smaller valleys, the countryside in central Tajikistan is more diverse than in the north. Several important rivers supply water to various human-made reservoirs or directly to the irrigated fields. High-altitude valleys and small canyons in the mountains are the sites of alpine forests and several national parks with picturesque landscapes. Other small valleys and hill groupings in central Tajikistan are dry and deserted due to water shortages or deforestation.

The largest city and the capital of the country, Dushanbe, is located in central Tajikistan. It grew from a small trading center at the turn of the 20th century into one of the largest cities in Central Asia by the beginning of the 21st century. However, rapid population growth in this part of the country brought about numerous environmental and social problems, which have required significant attention from the national government as well as assistance from the international community.

**THE SOUTHWESTERN REGION**    The region of Khatlon, with the provincial capital of Bokhtar (also known as Qurghonteppa), is the warmest part of the country. Its mild climate makes it ideal for growing cotton, vegetables, and other agricultural products. The Vakhsh and Panj river valleys are among the most productive lands in Tajikistan. These rivers begin as rushing streams high in the mountains and flow into the relatively low hills in the south. The banks and surrounding areas of these and other smaller rivers are famous for their *tugais*, dense forests made up of a variety of shrubs and trees.

The largest human-made reservoir, the Nurek, is located in this part of the country, preserving water for one of Central Asia's major hydroelectric power stations.

**THE EASTERN REGION**    The Gorno-Badakhshan Autonomous Region (or Kuhistanti Badakhshan Region) makes up the eastern part of the country. Its capital is Khorugh, near the border with Afghanistan. This is Tajikistan's frontier region, known for its cold continental climate and often inhospitable environment. The nation's highest mountains are located in Badakhshan. Many ranges rise higher than 16,000 feet (4,879 m) above sea level. Glaciers and permafrost cover the highest elevations. However, climate change is taking a toll on these glaciers. Scientists say the area of Tajikistan covered by glaciers has declined by 70 percent in as many years. Only the large ones remain— where once there were 14,000 glaciers, now there are only about 1,000.

Badakhshan makes up nearly half of the country, but it is sparsely populated since many parts of the region are inaccessible during winter and most of the small alpine valleys cannot sustain intensive agriculture. In fact, only 3 percent of the nation's people live in this region. Badakhshan is home to one of the largest religious minority groups in Central Asia—the Ismaili community, which has religious links with the Shiite Muslims of Iran.

## CLIMATE

Tajikistan's central location and close proximity to several vast mountain ranges shape its climate. The unique feature of Tajikistan's annual temperatures is that their fluctuation depends on the area's elevation above sea level and not necessarily on the season or time of the year. Therefore, some parts of northern Tajikistan are warmer than other areas to the south and east. In general, precipitation and temperatures vary widely both in summer and winter.

In the valleys of northern and central Tajikistan, the climate is relatively mild and dry. Temperatures range from 7 degrees Fahrenheit (-14 degrees Celsius) to 45°F (7°C) in January, and the average daily temperature is between 79°F (26°C) and 95°F (35°C) in July. In most of the valleys of southern Tajikistan, the climate is subtropical, with slightly warmer average temperatures.

An almost dry riverbed runs through the Wakhan Valley along the Pamir Highway in Tajikistan. The Hindu Kush mountains of Afghanistan can be seen in the background.

The weather in the mountains of eastern Tajikistan, however, is characterized by extremes. In the mountain ranges with low altitudes, the climate is drier, with temperatures ranging from 0°F (-18°C) to 41°F (5°C) in January and between 50°F (10°C) and 72°F (22°C) in July. The climate is more severe in the high Pamirs (13,120 feet—or 4,000 m—and higher), with temperatures dropping even lower. Rainfall varies between 7 inches (18 centimeters) in the northern and southern parts of the country and 40 to 50 inches (102 to 127 cm) in the central region. Tajikistan also possesses some of the most extensive water resources in Central Asia, stored in numerous mountain lakes, glaciers, and reservoirs.

Tajikistan has been affected by global warming and the drying up of the Aral Sea, located in Uzbekistan and Kazakhstan. Harsh droughts have plagued the Fergana Valley and vast areas of southern Tajikistan. In addition, summers are drier in central Tajikistan, and winters are much colder in the more mountainous parts of the republic. Deforestation of the mountain slopes has increased the risk of landslides across the nation as well. There have also been reports about the rapid shrinking of some of the glaciers in central and eastern Tajikistan.

*Tajikistan's Gorno-Badakhshan Province encompasses a large part of the Pamir Mountains. This mountain range sits at the junction of the Himalayas and the Tian Shan, Karakoram, Kunlan, Hindu Kush, and Hindu Raj ranges. Since they are among the earth's highest peaks, the Pamirs are often called the "Roof of the World."*

*Three of Tajikistan's highest peaks are in this eastern region: Ismoil Somoni Peak (formerly Communism Peak), 24,590 feet (7,495 m); Abu Ali Ibn Sino Peak (formerly and still often called Lenin Peak), 23,406 feet (7,134 m); and Peak Korzhenevskaya, 23,310 feet (7,105 m). When Tajikistan was a part of the Soviet Union, many of its mountains were given the names of Russian heroes, places, or principles. Upon becoming an independent nation, Tajikistan renamed some of those mountains, but the country's Pamir region still includes Russia Peak; Moscow Peak; Karl Marx Peak; Engels Peak; Peak of the Soviet Officers; Mayakovsky Peak, named for a Russian poet; and others that still reflect the nation's Soviet history.*

*Many glaciers cover the upper levels of the Pamirs, most notably the Fedchenko Glacier, named for a Russian explorer (though he was not someone who explored this glacier). This long, narrow glacier extends for around 48 miles (77 km) and is the longest one in the world outside of Earth's polar regions. Like many other glaciers, it is melting and retreating in the face of climate change.*

*The Tajik National Park encompasses most of the Pamir range, around 6.2 million acres (2.5 million hectares). The huge park includes around 1,085 glaciers, 170 rivers, and more than 400 lakes.*

## FLORA

Tajikistan is home to a diverse array of plants and trees, ranging from desert and steppe plants to alpine forests. Experts have identified more than 5,000 species of plants present in the nation.

Today, the native flora of the valleys and steppes has been largely replaced by many domesticated plants. Often, rows of cotton spread for acres, leaving little space for wild vegetation. The land along the roads and canals and around the cities and towns is often reserved for grape arbors as well as apple, pear, and apricot trees. Land along the banks of some rivers is covered with poplars, reeds, and plum grass. Collectively, they form the tugais, impenetrable tangles of shrubs, swamp grass, and trees. During recent decades, however, the tugais have nearly disappeared since farmers have cut down vast tracts of them to use the land for cultivation and grazing.

On the slopes of low-altitude mountains and hills, different types of plant life abound. Grains, potatoes, vegetables, and fruit trees replace the rows of cotton. Pistachios, Bukhara almonds, hawthorns, junipers, walnuts, wild apples, cherries, plums, and other shrubs and trees find refuge along the mountain rivers and creeks, forming small islands of natural habitat. Medieval histories report that about 1,000 years ago, large forests covered the slopes of numerous mountain ranges and hills in present-day Tajikistan. However, the local population reclaimed the land to cultivate various cash crops and used the forest as a source of fuel and wood for both construction and industry. Today, forests occupy less than 3 percent of the country, and they continue to shrink due to the lack of funding for preservation and reforestation activities.

The natural habitat has been largely preserved in the alpine areas, especially in the eastern parts of the country. Junipers, barberries, pistachios, and some other trees can be found in these areas. The pastures and open fields of the alpine areas are rich with grass during summer and are used for fattening large herds of domesticated sheep, especially a local breed of fine-fleece sheep.

Tajikistan's highest mountains have sparse vegetation, usually small bushes and grasses that can survive frigid winter temperatures.

## FAUNA

A wealth of animal life finds refuge in the valleys and forests and on the mountain slopes of Tajikistan. The nation's lowland hollows and dry steppes are home to many reptiles such as saw-scaled vipers, Egyptian sand boas, tortoises, and deadly Central Asian cobras. It is still common to see mammals

A snow leopard (*Panthera uncia*) is at home in the cold, mountainous terrain of Tajikistan.

such as porcupines, gerbils, and hamsters in open fields or on small hills. In the past, these areas were inhabited by the famous Central Asian gazelles, creatures that inspired many local poets and painters to use their images in famous works. However, the claiming of once-wild land for agriculture and uncontrolled hunting contributed to the near disappearance of these gorgeous animals by the beginning of the 21st century.

The forests that blanket the mountain slopes and the banks of many rivers are populated by Bukhara deer, jackals, leopards, wild boars, bears, wolves, and ibex. At higher altitudes, the alpine forest gives sanctuary to Siberian ibex, snow leopards, argalis, and numerous species of birds, including Himalayan and Tibetan snow cocks and golden eagles. In the nation's rockier regions, it is still possible to see the world's largest wild sheep, the Marco Polo sheep, whose nearly 3-foot (0.9 m) long outward-spreading horns were considered trophies prized by royalty and displayed in various palaces in Asia and Europe. Many Central Asian historians reported that the local rulers (begs and khans) used these forests as hunting grounds. However, in the 19th and 20th centuries, the areas of wild forest shrank significantly, and many animals were threatened with extinction. The risk persists. Experts estimate that only between 250 and 280 snow leopards are left in the wild in Tajikistan. About 140 of them live in Tajik National Park.

Various types of freshwater fish, including trout, carp, and common marinka, can be found in the country's many rivers, creeks, and lakes. Tajikistanis like to fish both for recreation and for personal consumption, but a commercial fishing industry has yet to be fully developed in the country.

## CITIES

Since ancient times, many small trading centers and cities have sprung up in the territory that is present-day Tajikistan. However, due to the numerous

the "old city," were destroyed in the medieval era or during the clashes of the 19th and 20th centuries.

Today, Kulob is a prominent agricultural center that specializes in cotton, grain, and food processing.

**KHORUGH** The capital of the Gorno-Badakhshan Autonomous Province, Khorugh is a city of about 30,000 people. Situated about 7,200 feet (2,195 m) above sea level, the city has one of the nation's highest elevations. Located on the banks of the Ghund River in eastern Tajikistan, Khorugh is a city with several small factories, a university, and a theater.

This aerial view shows the city of Khorugh, located near the border with Afghanistan.

## INTERNET LINKS

http://factsanddetails.com/Central-asia/Tajikistan/sub8_6e/entry-4898.html
This site offers many bulleted points of information about the geography of Tajikistan.

https://www.nytimes.com/2009/12/20/travel/20Pamir.html
This travel article brings Tajikistan's Wakhan Valley to life.

https://www.scmp.com/magazines/post-magazine/travel/article/2176702/tajikistans-pamir-mountains-road-trip-across-roof
This article depicts the writer's journey through the Pamir Mountains, with photos and a map.

https://whc.unesco.org/en/statesparties/tj
This is the UNESCO World Heritage page for Tajikistan.

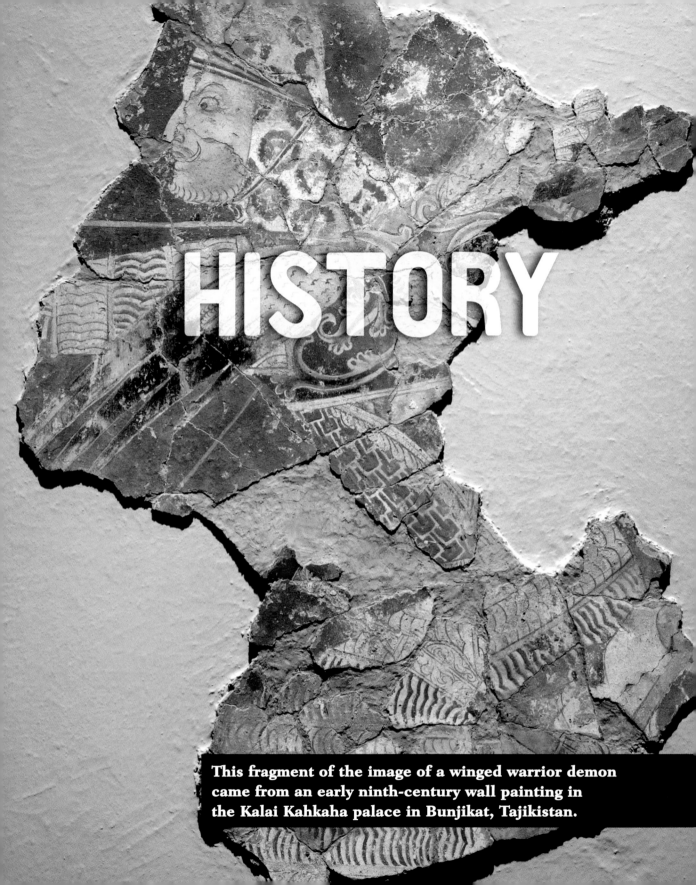

# HISTORY

This fragment of the image of a winged warrior demon came from an early ninth-century wall painting in the Kalai Kahkaha palace in Bunjikat, Tajikistan.

**2**

TAJIKISTAN IS AN ANCIENT PLACE but a young nation. It achieved its independence in 1991 after the breakup of the Soviet Union, but this land and its people have a long and fascinating history. The ancestors of the Tajiks lived for centuries in what are today Afghanistan, Kyrgyzstan, Tajikistan, and Uzbekistan, and their history is inseparable from that of the rest of Central Asia.

The Tajiks are descended from the Iranian peoples who formed ancient Bactria and Sogdiana—Central Asian civilizations from around 2500 BCE to 1000 CE)—bravely fighting the armies of Alexander the Great, the Persians, the Arabs, and centuries later, the hordes of Genghis Khan. Silk, handmade rugs, weaponry, jewelry, and many other products made by the skillful local craftspeople of these civilizations were prized not only across Central Asia, but also in many parts of China, India, Persia, the Middle East, and the Byzantine Empire.

Several factors contributed to the rise and fall of the ancient Central Asian civilizations. Fertile land, a mild climate, and an abundance of natural resources in the region provided local craftspeople with the necessary means of pursuing their trades. In addition, the people settled in towns that were on or near the great Silk Roads between Europe and China. The area became a melting pot of cultures, from the region's more established communities to the nomads who inhabited the Eurasian steppes.

Ancient ruins in Panjakent and Bunjikat, Tajikistan, have revealed murals and other artifacts dating from the pre-Islamic Sogdian civilization of Central Asia. The excavated sites are among the "Silk Road Sites in Tajikistan," which have been added to the tentative selections on UNESCO's World Heritage List.

# EARLY DAYS

Archaeologists have conducted major excavations of cities and towns that flourished from the eighth to the fourth centuries BCE in what is now Tajikistan. Piece by piece, they have uncovered the once-mysterious histories of the legendary Bactrian and Sogdian civilizations. Even so, many pages of those histories are still blank. People of this region most likely developed agriculture and industries in the eighth century BCE and became actively involved in a trade network. They also acquired military and administrative skills.

When Alexander the Great led his army into the region, he discovered prosperous cities, large and small, that had been integrated into a powerful Persian state and whose people followed the Zoroastrian religion. Alexander defeated the local resistance and left behind a small Greek-influenced colony. The ancient Greeks who remained in the region interacted with local residents, and the cultures of the two groups blended. Numerous remnants of the art of this era can be seen in local museums.

Bactria was destroyed in devastating wars in the second and first centuries BCE. After decades of war and other turbulent events, the area became a part of another powerful state—the Kushan Empire, which probably lasted until the late fourth or early fifth century CE. During this era, local people developed art and culture and established their own writing system based on the Greek and Aramaic alphabets. They built numerous canals for irrigation and constructed many urban areas. Some ancient sources called Bactria "the country of a thousand cities."

The people traded mostly with India, China, and the Roman Empire, traveling to different parts of the world and bringing home new ideas and beliefs. Also during this period, Buddhist, Manichaean, and Christian (mainly the Nestorian Eastern Church) religions spread in Central Asia, peacefully coexisting with Zoroastrian beliefs. In the fifth to the eighth centuries CE, unrest generally prevailed when the region entered another wave of turbulent wars and conflicts with various Turkic-speaking tribes that had arrived from east-central Asia.

*Zoroaster, also called Zarathustra, was a priest in Persia, but the dates of his life are uncertain. Scholars date his existence as being anywhere from 1500 BCE to 650 BCE or so. Not much is known about him or his life, but he had a powerful effect on history. He lived in a time when most religions were polytheistic; that is, people believed in many different gods. Zoroaster worked out a complex philosophy and religion based, instead, on*

Zoroaster speaks with the king of Persia in this painting from a Zoroastrian temple in Iran.

*monotheism, the belief in one god. He also developed the concept of dualism in religion—the belief that the universe is controlled by two forces—Good and Evil. This belief system influenced the development of Judaism, Christianity, and Islam.*

*Zoroaster is also said to have been one of the originators of astrology, the practice of reading cosmic signs as a way of predicting future events, and he is believed to have had a hand in developing the field of magic. He also influenced classical civilization in ancient Greece. The Greeks considered him a skilled healer, craftsman, and agriculturist, as well as an esteemed philosopher, mathematician, astrologer, and magician.*

*The Zoroastrian faith became the main religion of Persia (present-day Iran) until the emergence of Islam in the seventh century CE. Muslim persecution soon forced followers of the religion to flee. The largest numbers migrated to India where, in the Mumbai (formerly Bombay) region, they developed into a well-educated wealthy community known as the Parsees. Today, there are few, if any, followers of this religion in Tajikistan. However, it is an important part of the region's heritage, and Zoroastrian symbolism is depicted on the country's flag and in other cultural icons. Numerous Zoroastrian historical sites have been identified, mostly in the Gorno-Badakhshan region.*

## INVADERS

Between the sixth and eighth centuries CE, Central Asia underwent several fundamental changes. In the sixth century or probably even earlier, Turkic-speaking peoples began to arrive in the region in large numbers from their homelands in Siberia, Mongolia, and the northern steppes of China. They eventually took control of the entire Central Asian region, establishing vast but often unstable realms. These empires extended up to several million square miles. The nomads brought along not only their Turkic language and culture, but also their superb military organization and skills in warfare. Often, these newcomers settled close to Central Asian cities and towns, adopting local traditions and cultures while their rulers indulged themselves in the luxuries of life. Gradually, they lost their foothold in the region and were defeated by new conquerors. This political cycle would repeat itself time and again.

## ARRIVAL OF ISLAM

The second major change arrived from a very different direction and was in many ways more fundamental and profound. In the seventh and eighth centuries, the Muslim Arabs arrived in Central Asia to spread Islam, a religious system founded by the Prophet Muhammad. The Arabs conquered major cities in the region one by one and finally reached the western outskirts of the Chinese empire. In the decisive Battle of Talas in 751, the Arabs and the Chinese fought each other. Both armies suffered such huge losses that both were forced to retreat. Still, the conflict established a rough dividing line. For many centuries to come, the western outskirts of the Chinese empire became the boundary between the Islamic and Chinese worlds.

Initially, the local population resisted the Arabs, but gradually, over many decades, they began accepting Islam. The caliphs, or rulers of the Islamic world, encouraged the development of Islamic culture. However, they also tolerated other religions and cultures and supported numerous artists and scientists who arrived in the caliphate (Islamic empire) from around the world.

Central Asia became one of the strongholds of Islamic civilization, and Central Asians contributed significantly to the great achievements of the time.

# THE SILK ROAD: CROSSROADS OF EAST AND WEST

*In 138 BCE, when the Chinese general Chang Chien traveled west to the Fergana Valley in search of the powerful horses he had heard so much about, he did not realize he was establishing one of history's legendary trade routes.*

*The Silk Road, as it came to be called, was more than one route; it was a network, or corridor, of correlating trails that crossed the vast expanse of Central Asia. It linked East to West, connecting and opening up once-distant realms, hastening the exchange of their various goods, ideas, technologies, and religious beliefs.*

*Three major routes ran through present-day Tajikistan: the first was the Sogdian, or North route between Samarqand (in Uzbekistan) and Kashgar (in western China); the second one was Karategin route between Termez (in Uzbekistan) and Kashgar; and the third was the Pamir route linking Balkh (in Afghanistan) and Tashkurgan (in northwest China).*

*Along inhospitable mountain trails and across harsh plateaus, caravans would wind their way to the West, bringing silks, tea, spices, perfumes, medicines, paper, jade, porcelain, and dyes. The traders going east brought horses, camels and other animals; wine and grapes; linen and wool; glassware; weapons and armor; slaves; and gold and other precious metals.*

*The caravans also carried more than mere goods—the ideas, arts, religions, and technologies that were spread enriched both cultures. The East gained exposure to Christianity, Judaism, and the art and music of Europe. China received Nestorian Christianity (a branch of the faith that broke off from Byzantine Christianity in the 430s) and Buddhism (from India) via the Silk Road. Meanwhile, merchants spread Islam throughout the mountainous regions. The West learned about printing, paper money, and gunpowder.*

*Although the Silk Road waxed and waned as a route for transporting goods and ideas, it was revived in the 13th and 14th centuries with the travels of Marco Polo. A Venetian merchant, Marco Polo traveled along the Silk Road with camels laden with goods. Sea routes eventually proved more efficient, but the land routes still exist today in parts. Numerous remains of* caravanserais, *or caravan inns, shown here, can still be found in present-day Tajikistan.*

Tajik scholars believe that many of the best examples of early Tajik culture come from this era. For example, the poet Rudaki produced beautiful and fascinating verse; Firdawsi wrote his monumental *Shahnameh* (Book of Kings), a poetic chronicle of the Persian world; and Ibn Sina (also known as Avicenna) wrote his encyclopedic works on medicine, astronomy, and philosophy.

Then, between the 10th and 12th centuries, Central Asia began experiencing the first signs of decline. As the caliphate weakened and Central Asian states and principalities became politically divided, Central Asian rulers were increasingly involved in numerous internal wars as well as conflicts with the outside world. This further undermined their stability and unity, as new threats were rising from the East.

## INVADERS, AGAIN

Between 1219 and 1224, the Mongols, led by Genghis Khan, descended on the area, setting off the most devastating war in the region's history. These invaders conducted very brutal types of military campaigns.

Not only did they crush armies and destroy fortresses that attempted any form of resistance, they also massacred the residents of entire cities and

A restored 2,500-year-old fortress in Hisor, about 18 miles (29 km) west of Dushanbe, was a checkpoint on the Silk Road. It was supposedly captured and destroyed 21 times.

provinces, and they destroyed irrigation systems and vital infrastructure. A number of cities were burned to ashes, and many irrigated fields, farms, wineries, and gardens were turned into barren wastes. The devastation was so complete that many areas would never be able to reclaim their former glory.

Despite the rapid decline these campaigns set off in the region, the huge Mongol Empire—probably the largest in the medieval era—lasted only a few decades and experienced its own decline with the death of Genghis Khan and the intense strife among his successors.

## CHAOS AND TURMOIL

After the decline of the Mongol Empire, some local rulers in Central Asia such as Timur (Tamerlane) tried to revive past glories by waging new wars and spending handsomely on new fortresses, palaces, public buildings, and monuments. By the 17th and 18th centuries, though, most international traders avoided Central Asia, finding that sea routes from Europe to India and China were faster and safer.

Meanwhile, the Central Asian economies continued to be threatened by internal wars and rivalries and increased bandit activity. Roving thieves and hoodlums raided trade caravans or even small frontier cities and towns, capturing people who were then sold in slave bazaars across the region. In such an environment of chaos and turmoil, there was little technological innovation, since local economies remained significantly underdeveloped.

During this era, new powerful khanates, or principalities, emerged in the region: Bukhara, Kokand, and Chorasmia. They vigorously competed for political dominance in various parts of the region, including the land populated by the Tajiks' ancestors. They invested seemingly boundless economic and human resources in a succession of brutal wars.

## THE RUSSIAN EMPIRE

In the 19th century, a new superpower emerged to the north of Central Asia— the Russian Empire. The Russian czars and their administrations made clear their interest in developing trade relations with Central Asian khanates as well as in ending the slave trade in the region. In addition, czarist military ministers were interested in establishing military and diplomatic control of the area, as they became increasingly alarmed by the aggressive British takeover of the Indian subcontinent, Afghanistan, and Persia. During that time, very little was known in Russia and Europe about the khanates. Their cultures remained a mystery, and their supposed wealth became the focal point of numerous legends. Tales of diamonds, rubies, and hoards of gold hidden in palaces and the ruins of ancient cities were repeated again and again.

In the second half of the 19th century, the czarist army invaded Central Asia and, after several decisive battles, asserted control over most of the region. Still, it took about 30 years for the Russians to establish dominance over what today is Tajikistan, since some communities mounted significant resistance to the invaders. The czarist administration opted for diplomatic and military control over the region, and all middle- and high-level decisions were exclusively reserved for members of the vast colonial administration. However, the local administration was left intact, and some degree of political power remained in the hands of the area's original Central Asian inhabitants in order to pacify the local population. The judiciary system at the community level was also left in the hands of local judges (*qadis*), who dispensed justice according to Islamic law (*Shariah*).

On the economic front, the colonial administration introduced few restrictions and actively promoted trade between Russia and its Central Asian colonies. New railroad lines were built to Tashkent and Samarqand. This significantly increased trade volume in the region, and new small factories sprang up in major urban areas, especially those that processed cotton, one of the main export commodities of the region. Nevertheless, many parts of Central Asia experienced little social or cultural change and remained isolated from the outside world.

## THE BOLSHEVIKS AND THE SOVIET SYSTEM

The Bolsheviks, a political group that overthrew the ruling Russian regime in 1917, were locked in a bitter civil war for nearly five years. During this period, many parts of Central Asia regained a significant degree of autonomy, or

self-rule, from the Russian (or Soviet) authorities. It took until 1921 to 1922 for the Soviets to reestablish their control over most of Central Asia, but this control was often limited, especially in the Pamir Mountains and parts of the Fergana Valley.

In order to win political support from the populace, the Communist Soviet government entrusted many positions in the local and regional administration to the native intelligentsia (intellectuals) and professionals. After a few years of consultations and planning, the Tajik Soviet Socialist Republic was established in 1924, its borders officially set by Communist Party officials in Moscow. In 1929, it was granted the status of a union republic, becoming a main part of the Soviet Union, and was given control of the territory of the Leninabad (Sughd) province. The Communist Party of Tajikistan came to power and remained the single ruling party for the next 70 years.

Tajik women are seated on a carpet, with one playing a frame drum, in this photo from 1900.

This was the first time in the history of the Tajik people that they were recognized as a nation-state and were able to develop their own distinct and defined economy, education system, culture, language, and art. However, this development came at a price. Soviet authorities established firm control over the political, military, and diplomatic affairs of the republic. They endorsed a one-party political system and introduced heightened state control over economic development.

In addition, Soviet leaders banned private ownership of land and free entrepreneurship while nationalizing most of the industries and banks. Thousands of individuals who resisted the Soviet system were imprisoned, exiled to Siberia, or executed. All political and religious organizations, except the Bolshevik Party (eventually renamed the Communist Party) and its youth wing (called Komsomol), were banned. A Tajik government was in place, but it had little say in policy making, since it was obliged to get approval from the Soviet politburo (policy-making committee) for practically all political and economic decisions. No free discussions and no criticism of the Soviet system or of the Communist Party were permitted.

Only in the mid-1980s did the situation begin to change, as the liberal-minded Soviet leader Mikhail Gorbachev came to power and launched a program of greater freedom and openness called *perestroika*. The Tajik political leaders and intelligentsia seized the opportunity and began criticizing many aspects of the Soviet social and political system and its totalitarian control of Tajikistan. Gradually, some groups in Tajikistan began demanding full independence.

## INDEPENDENCE

The year 1991 became an important benchmark in the history of the Soviet Union and of Tajikistan in particular. Several republics of the Soviet Union seized the opportunity to declare independence from the Soviet Union, which itself broke apart in December 1991.

Tajikistan had declared its independence three months earlier in September 1991. The Tajik authorities immediately introduced many changes. They established control over the banking and financial systems of the republic and nationalized many industrial enterprises that had been under the control of Moscow in the past. They also established their own military and security forces.

## CIVIL WAR AND RECONCILIATION

A short time later, beginning in 1992, the political situation in the republic became increasingly unstable. This was due to the growing confrontation between the conservative Tajik government, dominated by former Communists, and members of the opposition front that included members of the liberal intelligentsia, democratic organizations, and Islamic groups.

As in many developing nations, the struggle for power and reform was complicated by regional rivalries that existed among several political clans. Soon, the political confrontation escalated into a devastating civil war, as both sides turned to violence, destroying property and kidnapping and killing opponents.

Tajikistani refugees return home after having fled the fighting between rebels and government forces in the 1990s.

According to some estimates, as many as 100,000 people were killed in the fighting, and about 200,000 refugees escaped to neighboring states. In addition, there were food shortages, outbreaks of typhoid, the tremendous destruction of roads and bridges, and the near collapse of the health and educational systems and the economy in general.

A rusty Tajik tank, abandoned during the civil war, sits in a field next to the Dushanbe–Khorog highway M41, in the Komsolomabad area of Tajikistan.

## PEACE ACCORD

It took several years before the rival factions were brought to a negotiating table under pressure from the United Nations (UN), the United States, and Russia, the core nation of the former Soviet Union. The intensive negotiations between the government, led by President Emomali Rahmonov, and the United Tajik Opposition (UTO), led by Said Abdullo Nuri, continued throughout 1996 and 1997. In 1997, a peace accord was signed and an agreement to share power was finally achieved. A percentage of the positions in the government, army, police, and local administration was reserved for each of the opposition groups. In exchange, all parties agreed to end hostilities and dismantle local militia and armed paramilitary units. All groups took part in the elections and established a reconciled and united governmental front.

## AUTHORITARIAN RULE

The years of political unrest left the economy in ruins and largely dependent on foreign aid. Meanwhile, Islamic fundamentalist forces (namely, the Taliban) had been growing in neighboring, war-torn Afghanistan. These Afghan extremists flowed into Tajikistan, staging attacks and disrupting government and commerce. Ruled mainly by regional warlords, Afghanistan developed as a global center for narcotics production, and Tajikistan soon became a major transit point for Afghan heroin and opium headed for markets in the West and elsewhere.

Determined to gain control over the warlords in his own nation, President Rahmon (he dropped the Russian-style *ov* suffix from his name in 2007) cracked down on political and religious opposition groups. His increasingly authoritarian rule led to changes in the constitution to allow him to extend his presidency indefinitely and to provide him with lifelong immunity from prosecution. Additional constitutional changes eased the way for Rahmon's son to succeed him and granted Rahmon the special status of "Leader of the Nation."

Tajikistan's President Emomali Rahmon waves during a welcoming ceremony in Dushanbe for Russian leader Vladimir Putin on February 27, 2017.

## INTERNET LINKS

**https://www.bbc.com/news/world-asia-16201087**
This BBC timeline provides a look at the history of Tajikistan, focusing mainly on the 20th and 21st centuries.

**https://www.britannica.com/place/Tajikistan**
This online encyclopedia tells the story of Tajikistan, including coverage of recent events.

**https://www.lonelyplanet.com/tajikistan/background/history/a/nar/e0f0e76b-32b0-4a40-8ca8-0080cee949ce/357579**
This travel site offers a succinct overview of Tajikistan's history.

**https://www.rferl.org/a/qishloq-ovozi-tajikistan-civil-war/28575338.html**
This article relates the story of the Tajikistan civil war.

# GOVERNMENT

The flag of independent Tajikistan preserved the red, green, white, and gold colors of the previous Soviet Tajik flag but changed the design and symbolism.

# 3

THE REPUBLIC OF TAJIKISTAN IS A presidential republic in which the president is both the head of state and the head of government within the framework of a multiparty system. Legislative power is vested in both the executive branch and the two chambers of the parliament.

In 1991, the former Tajik Soviet Socialist Republic declared its independence. Today, the nation celebrates that occasion on Independence Day, or National Day, on September 9. Tajikistan's modern governmental institutions and political culture developed under the overwhelming influence of the Soviet Union's ideology and political system. The political changes that were later brought about in the post-independence era significantly altered the ways in which the government functions.

After declaring independence, the conservative government at first resisted any kind of radical political and economic reforms and stuck to Soviet-era policies and views. In 1992, a civil war, fuelled by a regional rivalry and growing Islamic influence, broke out in Tajikistan, leading to the removal of President Rahmon Nabiyev. After numerous clashes between the government and the opposition, a coalition of regional leaders installed Emomali Rahmonov as the head of state.

One of the most important features of Tajikistan's system of government is the concentration of enormous influence and executive power in the hands of the president and his administration. The other notable feature is the relative weakness of political parties and the sustained strength of groups built around regional political networks. Tajiks often support and vote for political leaders based on candidates' regional or local affiliation and rarely on their political views.

In 1994, Rahmonov won the presidential election. Then, in 1997, after the government signed a peace accord with the United Tajik Opposition (UTO), several government positions were filled with UTO supporters. In a bitterly contested presidential election in 1999, the UTO candidate lost to Rahmonov, who has held the post ever since. (In 2007, he changed his name to Rahmon.)

## THE CONSTITUTION

National constitutions can be beautiful things. These official documents lay the legal foundation upon which a government and society will function. They often describe a system that reveres human rights, freedoms, and justice within the construct of a country's particular culture. The texts inevitably declare the source of the government's power to be grounded in the people and go on to lay out a foundation of ideals. However, the extent to which any nation's political reality reflects the constitutional ideal is a matter of how vigorously those ideals are enforced. Most nations naturally have some gap between the ideal and the actual, and in Tajikistan's case, it's quite a wide one.

Tajikistan's newest constitution was introduced in 1994, replacing the Soviet constitution of 1978. According to the document, Tajikistan is a secular state; officials have repeatedly rejected demands from some religious groups to declare Tajikistan an Islamic state or to introduce an Islamic legal system. Indeed, Article 8 states, "Religious unions are separate from the State and may not interfere with State affairs."

The constitution grants freedoms to independent media and various political organizations, and it prohibits discrimination or persecution of women, ethnic minorities, and religious groups. It also recognizes the division of powers among the judicial, executive, and legislative branches of government. In reality, however, this system of checks and balances is not really effective, since much of the power is concentrated disproportionately in the hands of the executive branch.

By the mid-20th century, Tajikistan was the second-largest cotton producer in the Soviet Union and among the top 10 producers in the world. What is called the monoculture of cotton—focusing on this single crop at the expense of all other agricultural products—led to several negative consequences. Farmers became extremely dependent on the decisions of the state institutions that controlled agricultural policies and funding. This reliance made farmers extremely vulnerable to external economic shocks.

It also rapidly increased the use of fresh water for irrigation, leading to the depletion of water reserves not only in Tajikistan but throughout Central Asia. In addition, excessive irrigation led to the salinization and the depletion of soil in many places, reducing productivity or making land unusable for commercial agriculture. In the 1990s, many farmers experienced great losses, since the government hastily cut off most of its agricultural funding at the same time a collapse in cotton prices gripped the international market.

A woman collects cotton in a field near the village of Navobod.

*Tajikistan's shared border with Afghanistan exposes it to some of the problems that afflict that war-torn country. For one thing, Tajikistan is one of the world's highest volume illicit drug-trafficking routes, functioning as a conduit between Afghan opiate production to the south and the illicit drug markets of Russia and eastern Europe to the north. Afghanistan is the world's leading producer of opium, a highly addictive drug derived from the opium poppy plant. The illicit drug heroin is derived from opium and is around two to three times more potent.*

*While there is no proof that the government is complicit in the underground smuggling trade, Tajikistan's Drug Control Agency interrupts only a tiny fraction of the trade. Some economists and other international observers think Tajik government officials personally rely on drug trafficking and profit off it themselves, but the nation as a whole also benefits from its stabilizing effects on the poor economy. The lack of jobs forces some Tajikistanis to take part in the black market by smuggling of drugs and other illicit goods. Indeed, heroin trafficking in Tajikistan is estimated to be the equivalent of 30 to 50 percent of the national GDP. In other words, the black market may well be subsidizing the official, lgeal economy.*

## MINING AND MANUFACTURING

Before the Soviet takeover, there were few manufacturing plants in the country. During World War II (1939–1945), the Soviet government relocated a number of factories from Nazi-occupied territories to Tajikistan. The move helped establish new industries, including defense manufacturing, the production of agricultural and industrial machinery, food processing, textile and garment manufacturing, and the mining of nonferrous metals. Tajikistan has rich deposits of gold, silver, and antimony. It also has a large-scale aluminum manufacturing sector that depends on imported ore.

The state-controlled development of the manufacturing sector led to several problems. First, state-owned enterprises were often inefficient and not competitive in the international market. Second, the aggressive development of land for industrial use led to severe environmental problems, including the erosion of the fragile soil found in mountainous oases and valleys. Thus, many industrial enterprises, unable to compete with foreign goods after the opening of the national market in the 1990s, were closed or experienced significant losses.

The Soviets also made significant investments into the construction of huge hydroelectric power stations. The Nurek Dam on the Vakhsh River, for example, is the second tallest human-made damn in the world, and its reservoir is the largest in Tajikistan. Built from 1972 to 1980 and renovated in 1988, the power station still creates much of the country's electricity. There are also six other hydroelectric stations in the country, with two on the Syr Darya River and the rest on the Vakhsh.

In 1976, the nation began construction of the Rogun Dam, also on the Vakhsh River. Construction was interrupted by historical events, but in 2016, the state commission in charge of the project contracted the Italian company Salini Impregilo to proceed with the construction for $3.9 billion. When completed, the proposed 1,099-foot (335 m) high dam will surpass the Nurek Dam, and will be the highest and tallest dam in the world. The project will include the building of six hydroelectric generating units with a power capacity totaling 3,600 megawatts. Construction is expected to be completed in 2028. In time, Tajikistan hopes to export more electricity to neighboring Uzbekistan from the Rogun plant; however, those export revenues are unlikely to make up for the huge costs of building the project.

## INTERNET LINKS

**https://carnegieendowment.org/2016/02/01/tajikistan-at-twenty-five-rahmon-consolidates-power-pub-62630**
This article from 2016 provides insight into a broad range of economic and political issues in Tajikistan.

**https://www.worldbank.org/en/country/tajikistan/overview#1**
The World Bank provides an overview and projection for Tajikistan's economy.

# ENVIRONMENT

Marco polo sheep are rare animals
that call Tajikistan home.

LIKE ALL COUNTRIES, TAJIKISTAN faces environmental challenges. Some problems, such as pollution, can be alleviated with sufficient political will, legislation, and enforcement. Others require cleanup of unsound environmental decisions made decades ago. Still others, such as climate change, can only be anticipated, managed, and adapted to at best. All of these approaches require governmental financial commitments, which so far, have been insufficient.

People have lived in Tajikistan for thousands of years, finding ways to eke a living out of the land. The situation has changed, though, during the last two centuries. The population of the country grew dramatically, increasing demands for water, arable land, and other resources.

In addition, the development of industry, mining, and widespread farming, especially in the 20th century, brought pollution and damage to the natural environment in many parts of the country, especially in the densely populated valleys and districts around the largest cities.

Recently, industrial pollution and global warming have led to the shrinking and eventual disappearance of some mountain glaciers, thereby decreasing freshwater reserves. Human activity continues to

> Tajikistan does not have a national waste management strategy and has not instituted a recycling program. Modernization of waste collection and disposal services, along with public education about recycling, is one of the country's urgent environmental needs.

negatively affect the wildlife in many parts of the country as well as the delicate environmental balance of the nation's various habitats.

As a developing nation, Tajikistan has few resources for dealing with its various ecological problems. In addition, most Tajikistanis live in rural areas. In times of economic hardship or drought, the rural population often exploits and overly stresses natural resources to supplement its daily needs. This is particularly seen in the deforestation of rural areas where the residents cut trees for heating and cooking fuel.

In recent decades, the government of Tajikistan, along with international organizations and nongovernmental organizations (NGOs), has introduced various projects aimed at preserving the nation's natural resources. For example, officials work intensively with farmers, hunters, herders, and many others to educate them about the importance of responsibly using and maintaining Tajikistan's valuable natural resources.

## FRAGILE MOUNTAIN ECOSYSTEM

About 93 percent of Tajikistan is covered with mountains. In fact, very tall mountains—more than 3,000 feet (914 m) above sea level—occupy more than 70 percent of the country. Tajikistan is home to many small and large valleys, canyons, and mountain slopes with unique landscapes and distinctive ecosystems.

The mountain ecosystems are very fragile, and damage done by humans often takes a long time to heal. In some cases, the effects are irreversible. For example, due to the harsh climate of the mountains, many types of trees and shrubs grow slowly, and it sometimes takes several decades before they reach their full growth. However, they could easily be wiped out in a matter of a few hours by accidental fires, by floods, or by local farmers who cut them for fuel or building materials.

Tajikistan possesses nearly 70 percent of Central Asia's glaciers and about 40 percent of its clean water reserves. The glaciers have been affected not only by global warming but, to a large extent, by the direct actions of people

as well. Trash left behind by tourists and hikers often contains lead, mercury, and other harmful substances that pollute the mountains' water reserves.

As of now, the government of Tajikistan has yet to turn its attention to some of the nation's most pressing environmental concerns. Preserving wildlife, protecting the alpine forests and tugais, and ensuring that the nation has a clean and sustainable water supply are just a few of its top priorities.

This glacier is one of many among the peaks of the Pamirs.

## DEFORESTATION AND WILDLIFE

One of Tajikistan's most serious environmental crises is the uncontrolled cutting of alpine forests for wood in order to heat homes in winter or to construct new

Pistachio trees such as these grow in southern Tajikistan.

houses. In addition, pistachio, Bukhara almond, and hedge rose trees, among others, have been overharvested, cut down for their nuts and berries. During the last 100 to 150 years, nearly 50 to 60 percent of the native forests have been lost, including magnificent groves of walnut, fig, and wild pomegranate trees.

In recent years, poaching and commercial hunting have emerged as major threats, not only to the wildlife of Tajikistan but also to the delicate ecological balance in the alpine zones. For example, the number of goitered gazelles living in the Tigrovaya Balka preserve has declined during the last three decades to the point where the gazelle is almost extinct. The threats to the populations of wildcats, foxes, wolves, and other animals cause disruptions in the food chain. These animals are key predators of the rats, mice, and birds that, when uncontrolled, damage the woodland and agricultural crops.

## RAMSAR SITES

*The Ramsar Convention on Wetlands is an international treaty for the conservation and sustainable use of wetlands. The treaty dates to 1971 and is named for the Iranian city of Ramsar where it was signed. The Convention uses a broad definition of wetlands— it includes all lakes and rivers, underground aquifers, swamps and marshes, wet grasslands, peatlands, oases, estuaries, deltas and tidal flats, mangroves and other coastal areas, coral reefs, and all human-made sites such as fish ponds, rice paddies, reservoirs, and salt pans.*

*Wetlands are of vital importance, according to the Convention, because they are among the world's most productive environments. They are ecosystems of "biological diversity that provide the water and productivity upon which countless species of plants and animals depend for survival."*

*As part of its mission, the convention identifies wetlands sites around the world that are of international importance and works to protect them. Of the 2,341 Ramsar sites (as of 2019), Tajikistan has five, covering a total of 233,762 acres (94,600 ha): Karakul, a lake in the Tajik National Park in the Pamir Mountains; the Kayrakum Reservoir, the large artificial lake created by the Kayrakum Dam in northwestern Tajikistan; the lower part of the Panj River, which forms much of the border between Tajikistan and Afghanistan; the Rangkul Valley Important Bird Area, in the eastern part of the country, not far from the border with China; and Zorkul, a lake in the Pamir Mountains on the border between Afghanistan and Tajikistan. The lake's northern half lies in Tajikistan, where it is protected as part of the Zorkul Nature Reserve.*

## WATER PROBLEMS

Irrigation and drinking water are key concerns in Tajikistan. There has been a sharp increase in water consumption in recent decades, combined with years of drought, which has compromised irrigation systems and reduced the supply of drinking water.

The conflicting needs of the agricultural and industrial sectors make water-use management all the more difficult. Hydroelectric power stations store millions of gallons of water in summer, releasing most of it in winter to

The Nurek Dam, with its hydroelectric station on the Vakhsh River, is the second-tallest dam in the world. Built between 1961 and 1980 by the Soviets, it rises 980 feet (300 m) high.

generate additional power for heating purposes. On the other hand, farmers need water in summer for irrigation, especially on large cotton and rice plantations, and if too much water is released in winter, fields could be flooded and arable land eroded.

Erosion is another serious problem. Deforestation often results in the soil being easily washed away, not only during the rainy season but after the snow melts as well. The problem is even graver in the more mountainous regions. It may take just a few days of heavy rain to strip hundreds of acres of land of its soil, while it takes decades or even centuries to restore the fertile topsoil in the alpine zones. In some areas, poor farmers burn vegetation on mountain slopes to prepare the land for planting cash crops. Too often, after a few rainy seasons, the soil is washed away and the newly cleared patches are deserted. In the end, the land undergoes major changes for very limited returns.

## CONSERVATION

Tajik scientists and conservationists understood the importance of preserving the natural environment long ago. The national Academy of Sciences, with government funding, launched several projects to educate people and encourage environmentally conscious industrial and agricultural undertakings. The oldest initiatives, the Tigrovaya Balka and Ramit wildlife preserves, were set up in the mid-20th century. About a dozen other wildlife sanctuaries were set up in the country at around the same time. In addition, there are three botanical gardens that serve as important centers for studying biodiversity in Tajikistan and ways of preserving the nation's growing list of endangered species.

## INTERNET LINKS

**https://blog.nationalgeographic.org/2014/06/11/tajikistan-brings-endangered-wild-goat-from-the-edge-of-extinction-to-the-peak-of-hope**
This *National Geographic* article discusses threats to the markhor (wild goat) population in Central Asia.

**https://www.unece.org/fileadmin/DAM/env/epr/epr_studies/ECE.CEP.180.Eng.pdf**
The United Nations Economic Commission for Europe
2017 Environmental Performance Review for Tajikistan reports in depth on the country's environmental progress.

**https://wwf.ru/en/resources/news/tsentralnaya-aziya/pervyy-mesyats-na-vole**
This short WWF article examines a project to reintroduce goitered gazelles to the Tigrovaya Balka preserve.

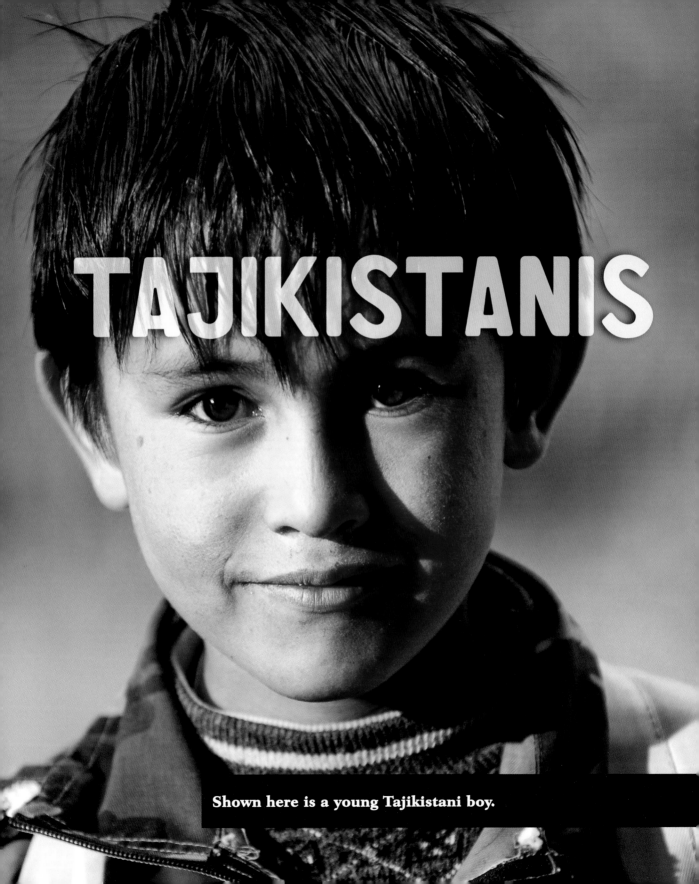

# TAJIKISTANIS

Shown here is a young Tajikistani boy.

**T**AJIKS ARE THE ETHNIC GROUP THAT makes up about 84 percent of the population of Tajikistan. The others are mostly Uzbeks, Kyrgyz, Russians, Turkmen, Tatars, and Arabs. Tajikistanis are all citizens of the nation of Tajikistan, regardless of ethnicity.

For centuries, the region that makes up present-day Tajikistan has been populated by various ethnic and religious groups. The groups that played the largest role in forming modern Tajikistani culture spoke Persian and Turkic-based languages. The Persian-speaking peoples established their presence and developed their cities first. The Turkic-speaking peoples began arriving in large numbers from the fourth to sixth centuries CE, probably even earlier.

In spite of religious, linguistic, and cultural differences, the various people who settled in the region cooperated with one another in times of foreign invasion or in the face of natural calamities such as earthquakes, floods, or droughts. There were significant cultural exchanges between the Persian- and Turkic-speaking communities, and intermarrying between the two groups became common. At the same time, some groups and communities competed fiercely with one another for political and economic influence or dominance. The area experienced its share of turbulent times, as a series of devastating wars slowed the consolidation of the Tajik nation and further weakened the people's abilities to resist foreign invaders.

By the late 19th century, the Russian Empire controlled most of the Central Asian region, but in many places, its presence was minimal. In the

A Tajikistani family poses with their motorcycle in the Pamir Mountains. The Russian-made Ural brand of motorcycles are a common form of transportation in the country.

20th century, however, the Soviet authorities established tighter control over the social and cultural aspects of the people living in Central Asia. When the boundaries of the Tajik state were drawn, many Tajik communities remained outside the country's official boundaries, mainly in the provinces of Bukhara and Samarqand in Uzbekistan. At that time, in the late 1920s, when the modern borders of Tajikistan were established, the population was about 1.2 million.

In 2020, the population of the country was estimated to be about 8.87 million. Tajikistan is one of the least urbanized countries on the Asian continent, with only around 27.5 percent of its people living in urban areas. Dushanbe is home to around 900,000 people, or just over 10 percent of the population. Tajikistan has one of the fastest-growing populations of the former Soviet states, and it is predicted that its population could double within the next 20 to 25 years.

# TAJIKS

Scholars still dispute the origins of the Tajik people, their cultural heritage, and even the origin of the word "Tajik." Some scholars translate the word Tajik as "crown," while others believe that it was probably just the name of a medieval tribe. Nevertheless, there is some consensus about the origin of the Tajik people.

Most Tajik scholars believe that the Tajik ancestors lived in what is now Afghanistan, Kyrgyzstan, Tajikistan, and Uzbekistan after about 2,000 BCE. The scholars claim that these predecessors had direct links to the populace of ancient Sogdiana and Bactria and the early Parthian states. The name Tajik did not emerge until much later, sometime around the 11th century.

Starting in ancient times, three different groups came together to form the Tajik nation. The first was the Persian-speaking population of the Pamir Mountains and the surrounding area. The second was a Turkic-speaking population grouped mostly in large and small cities and towns in the Syr Darya, Zeravshan, Vakhsh, and Panj river valleys. From medieval times on, the Persian-speaking population interacted closely with the Turkic-speaking people who arrived in the region in several small and large waves. By the 19th and 20th centuries, it was quite common for many families to be bilingual. They spoke Tajik, which is close to the dialect of Persian spoken in Iran, as well as various dialects of the Turkic languages. In the past, the Tajiks adopted Arabic script and used it until the early 20th century. The contemporary Tajik alphabet is based on Cyrillic script.

Arabs made up the third group that formed the Tajik nation. In the seventh and eighth centuries CE, the Arabs introduced Islam to the area, and gradually, a majority of the population abandoned Zoroastrianism, Buddhism, and Manichaeism for the newly imported faith. Today, most Tajiks belong to the Sunni school of Islamic thought, unlike the Iranians, who mostly belong to the other main branch of Islam, Shia.

According to government estimates, there are about 7.5 million ethnic Tajiks in the country. A significant number of Tajiks live outside Tajikistan, in parts of Afghanistan, Iran, Kyrgyzstan, and Russia.

## UZBEKS

Uzbeks make up Tajikistan's largest ethnic minority, accounting for about 13.8 percent of the population in 2014, which is when the most recent data was collected. They live in all parts of the country west of Badakhshan, but the largest enclaves are in the Fergana Valley. The Uzbeks speak a language belonging to the Turkic language group; it is different from the Tajik language, though many Uzbeks speak both languages.

The Uzbeks trace their origin to the Turkic-speaking group that began forming its own distinct language and culture, probably in the 15th and 16th centuries. The Uzbek tribal leaders led several wars to defend their land against the aggression of the Persian shahs and succeeded in establishing independent states. With the creation of the various Soviet republics in the 1920s, a majority of Uzbeks found themselves living in the newly established republic of Uzbekistan. However, small communities of Uzbeks remained in all the other Central Asian republics, including Tajikistan.

The Uzbeks maintain close relations within their communities, but they do not isolate themselves from the rest of the populace. They also play an important role in the political life of Tajikistan, since several ministerial positions in the national government are traditionally filled by ethnic Uzbeks. The Uzbeks did not participate actively in the civil war in the 1990s, but they did play a significant role in the reconciliation process.

## RUSSIANS

Russians, whose language belongs to the Slavic language group, constitute the second-largest ethnic minority in the country, though their numbers have steadily declined since 1991. They first arrived in Tajik-populated areas in the second half of the 19th century. Initially, most of them were Russian imperial troops stationed in strategic cities and towns throughout the region. Then, on the eve of the 20th century, several thousand Russian peasant families arrived in Central Asia in order to escape the poverty and economic hardship of life in Russia.

*Children are generally received with happiness in Tajikistan. Families with 6, 7, and even 10 children are common. In 2020, the birth rate was 21.8 births per 1,000 people,*

*ranking Tajikistan 68th in the world out of 229 nations. In general, poorer countries tend to have higher birth rates. This rate of births was greater than the death rate in Tajikistan for the same time period (5.8 deaths per 1,000 people) and reflects a relatively young median age of 25.3 years in the country. The population growth rate was 1.52 percent. (For comparison, the birth rate in the United States that year was 12.4 births per 1,000 people; the median age was 38.5 years; and the population growth rate was 0.72 percent.)*

*For Tajikistan, this means children and young people make up a large percentage of the population. Since most of those people are still economically dependent on their families and other members of society, a disproportionately youthful country means a significant portion of people are not yet in the labor force and therefore not contributing to the economy. Countries with a young population need to direct more of their resources to education, but with Tajikistan being such an economically poor country, it follows that the education system is sorely underfunded.*

members. Marriage also symbolizes independence and gaining a voice in the extended family and the community. In addition, marriage is considered to be a personal achievement for the parents of the bride and groom, since it often seals a union or partnership between the two families and ensures the continuation of two honorable and respected lineages.

In light of this, choosing a marriage partner is critical. Traditionally, when young people have reached marrying age or express a desire to establish a family of their own, all close and distant relatives are put on alert. Family and

A veiled bride takes part in an outdoor wedding ceremony in Hisor.

community members, friends, and colleagues are given the task of finding an appropriate spouse. They regularly organize various events and often set up "accidental" meetings between prospective partners. Even professional matchmakers are regularly called for help.

Often, the search is a short one, since parents might arrange a marriage themselves, choosing a partner they consider to be the most appropriate for their child. However, the young people usually have the final say and may accept the arranged marriage or introduce to their parents a person they prefer instead. Traditionally, it is expected that the family of the bridegroom pay a *kalym*, an offering in the form of money or gifts, to the family of the bride. The size of the kalym can vary and can become a substantial burden to the family.

Young people who marry are expected to stay together for life. However, divorce is allowed by Tajikistani civil law, and either partner can file for divorce. Under the current legal system, children of divorced parents usually remain with their mother, and the father is obliged to provide financial support for them until they reach the age of 18. In general, divorced people can remarry, though it is sometimes easier in urban environments than in rural areas.

Same-sex marriage is not legal in Tajikistan, and the social and political atmosphere for LGBTQ+ people in the country is quite hostile.

## NATIONAL TRADITIONS AND SOCIAL BEHAVIOR

In the past, traditional Tajik social relations were built around the concept of social and political rank and the separation of the sexes. The economic and political developments of the 20th century, however, significantly changed these notions. This has led to a complex mixture of past and present, a vibrant interchange between traditional Islamic and Central Asian culture and modern Western models.

The urbanization and modernization that characterized much of the 20th century left their imprint on national traditions, making them less restrictive and more flexible. More recently, the opening of the country to the outside world after its independence and the explosion of an international mass-media culture have contributed to major cultural shifts in Tajikistan. Young people have more independence and freedom, although tradition remains an important means of binding society.

Elderly people are considered to be a source of wisdom. They exert a strong influence both in their families and in their local communities. It is considered polite to listen to elders; to invite them for discussions of various social, political, and community matters; and to ask for their opinions about a wide variety of issues. Young people still go to the elderly members of their extended families and of their communities to ask for approval of major undertakings, such as decisions to move to other places or to accept work in other countries. This approval and advice, however, is not binding and does not carry the same weight it did about a half century ago. Still, elders often play a central role at the local level, and sometimes they are even entrusted to carry out justice in cases involving minor offences.

Until the 20th century, Tajik tradition strongly endorsed separating the sexes in public and family life. It was widely accepted that girls should be taught to be housewives only and to be prepared exclusively to perform domestic duties. Many women remained uneducated, because there was a strong traditional perception that they did not need extensive schooling. Women could not take positions in government or public life and could not vote or participate in any discussion of development at the community level. Moreover, they were not allowed to go out of their homes alone, even for shopping, especially without being properly veiled and dressed. Most houses were divided into separate sections for males and females, and the sexes could not mix in public even during weddings and other major family events.

In the late 1920s, the Soviet authorities introduced and fiercely enforced a policy of liberalization of women. They allowed women to abandon veiling in public. Women were encouraged to enroll in schools and universities and to serve in public positions. The government even established informal job quotas for women in universities, local and national governments, ministries, and the agencies that made up the Communist Party.

By the late 20th century, this policy had resulted in the creation of a large class of professional women, who had their own independent incomes and a strong presence in public institutions and many levels of government. Segregation of men and women in public was completely abandoned, and young people could meet at restaurants, nightclubs, sports centers, and other public places without any social stigma.

The situation began to change after 1991, as the steep economic recession, the civil war, and isolation from the outside world resulted in a high level of unemployment. Women were among the first to lose their jobs and their voices in public life. Some older, premodern traditions also have made a comeback in many parts of the country. Segregation of women and men in public, for example, has begun to slowly re-emerge during the last few decades.

Today, urban women still enjoy a large degree of freedom; they can decide on their own education, jobs, and lifestyles. Many young women in cities often prefer to wear Western-style dress and enjoy Western-style entertainment. Meanwhile, many rural women are often strongly encouraged not to attend school beyond the primary or secondary level and to prepare themselves almost solely to be housewives. In some families, girls' opinions are not counted when their families choose their future husbands, and young women are not allowed to go out alone without guardians.

## EDUCATION

Education is highly valued in Tajik society. In the past, it was the only means of overcoming social barriers and climbing the social ladder. After the Bolshevik revolution in Russia and the civil war of 1917 to 1922, a whole generation of policy makers, administrators, professionals, and artists rose to power and fame completely because of the personal abilities and talents they acquired and developed through good education. People in Tajikistan today undergo considerable hardships in order to provide their children with a good education at the best universities. It is quite common for an entire extended family to share the responsibility of raising the money needed to support children studying at prestigious universities in the capital city or overseas.

The education system in Tajikistan has a strong Russian influence. During the Soviet era, a modern education system provided free schooling to all children, with an emphasis on the sciences, mathematics, and practical day-to-day skills. By the 1940s, the government had eradicated mass illiteracy. According to official statistics, in 1989, more than 1.3 million students (approximately 23 percent of the population) attended 3,100 schools. In addition, 41,700 students attended 42 specialized secondary schools.

After 1991, schools in Tajikistan underwent two major changes. First, there was a greater emphasis on the use of the Tajik language as the medium of instruction. Second, as a consequence of the 1992 to 1997 civil war, there was a considerable withdrawal of state funding normally intended for education. The war left around 55,000 children orphaned, and at least 126 schools were totally destroyed. Many others were in need of repairs.

Girls attend class at a local school in rural Tajikistan.

In the 21st century, the government began to increase spending on education, raising teacher salaries by 25 percent in 2005. The Tajik language is now the primary language of instruction, but in 2003, Russian instruction was mandated as a second language in secondary school. Although the Tajikistanis have a nearly 100-percent literacy rate, the overall quality of public education is said to be low, hampered by an insufficient number of qualified teachers, poor infrastructure dating from the Soviet era, and a high dropout rate in secondary school.

The constitution of Tajikistan, adopted in 1994, states that general education is compulsory and free and that the state guarantees access to general, vocational, specialized, and higher education in state-controlled educational establishments. At age 7, children begin an 11-year compulsory education program, consisting of 4 years of primary school and 7 years of secondary school.

## URBANIZATION AND MIGRATION

Urbanization was a relatively recent concept for Tajikistan, since most cities and industrial centers grew rapidly only between the 1940s and 1980s. High levels of economic growth contributed to the creation of a large number of jobs in urban areas. This provided incentives for many people to move to the cities not only from the Tajik *kishlaks* (villages) but also from other rural areas of the Soviet Union. The urban population grew from 10 percent in 1924 to 35 percent in the 1970s. The development of a modern school system contributed further to a significant influx of people in the cities, because most talented young students received state scholarships to study at universities in Dushanbe. Those attending other universities in Central Asia and Russia often returned to the nation's urban centers after completing their coursework, in search of jobs and professional success.

Generally throughout the Soviet era, however, the government heavily regulated the country's population movement, trying to avoid an uncontrolled influx of unskilled labor into the large cities. People could not move until they received special registration permits called *propiska*. Due to these restrictions and a lack of industrial skills, many Tajiks preferred to remain in their rural communities. The government also provided large subsidies to the agricultural industry in order to sustain the large rural population.

The situation changed abruptly after 1991. The government cut off the agricultural subsidies, and Tajik farmers lost their access to the Russian market. These and some other factors made farming unprofitable in many parts of the country. The civil war and the political instability that followed only aggravated the economic situation. Not only did many people lose their jobs and incomes, but they also lost their land and, in some extreme cases, all their property. Tens of thousands of families moved to the metropolitan areas or even abroad to countries such as Kazakhstan, Iran, and Russia. According to various estimates, between 500,000 and 800,000 people, or between 12 and 18 percent of the population, moved from Tajikistan to other nations. It made Tajikistan one of the largest contributors of immigrants to all the republics that made up the former Soviet Union. In 2020, the net migration rate was estimated to be 1.1 migrants—or people who leave the country to live elsewhere—per 1,000 people.

## INTERNET LINKS

**https://www.advantour.com/tajikistan/traditions.htm**
This travel site provides information about Tajikistan's social rituals and traditions.

**https://www.cia.gov/library/publications/the-world-factbook/geos/ti.html**
The CIA *World Factbook* has up-to-date statistics related to the lifestyle of Tajikistanis.

**http://maorif.tj**
This is the official site of Tajikistan's Ministry of Education and Science, which is available in English.

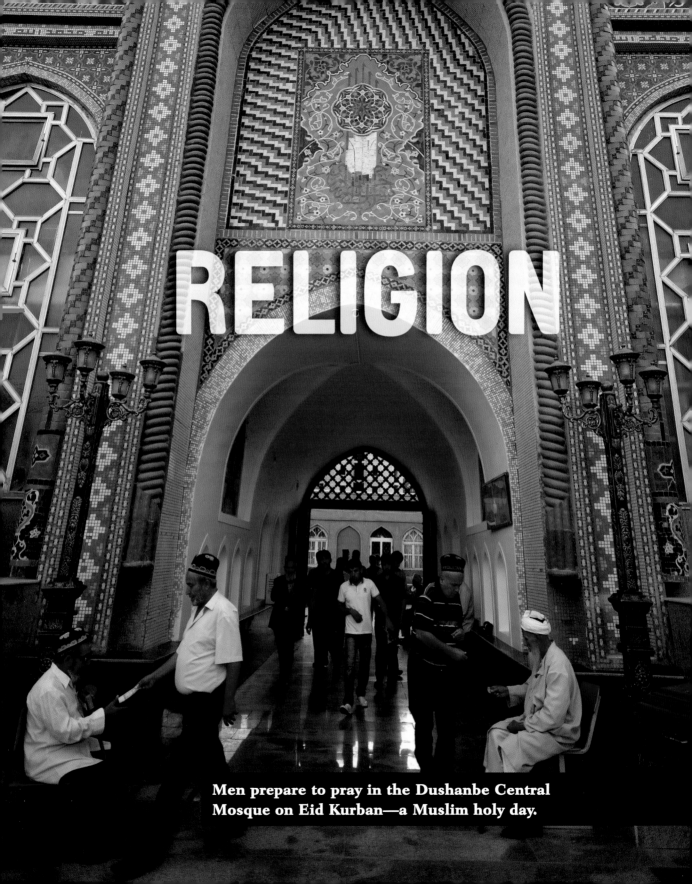

# RELIGION

**Men prepare to pray in the Dushanbe Central Mosque on Eid Kurban—a Muslim holy day.**

## 9

**T**AJIKISTAN'S OFFICIAL LANGUAGE IS Tajik, a dialect of Persian that is very similar to Farsi, the official language of Iran. Other languages used here include Uzbek, Kyrgyz, and Russian. The Uzbeks, who live mainly in northern Tajikistan, speak Uzbek, which belongs to the Turkic language group and is very different from Tajik. Turkic languages are spoken mainly in Central Asia, western China, Turkey, and some parts of Russia and Iran. Through centuries of cultural interaction, the language of Tajikistan's Uzbek population has absorbed many words of Tajik origin. There are also small communities of Kyrgyz people and Turkmens who speak their native languages, which also belong to the Turkic language group but are quite different from Uzbek. Russian-speaking people are also found in Tajikistan but in small numbers.

Uzbek is the second most widely spoken language in Tajikistan, used by about 12 percent of the population. In Tajikistan, Uzbek is written in the Cyrillic script, unlike in neighboring Uzbekistan, where it is written in a modified Latin alphabet.

Many people in Tajikistan are bilingual or even trilingual. It is common to hear Tajiks speaking Uzbek and Russian in addition to their native tongue. At the beginning of the 21st century, a new trend emerged in Dushanbe and other metropolitan areas as many young people began studying English. In addition, Arabic has gained popularity in many small towns and cities, especially among devoted Muslims. However, Tajik remains the lingua franca, the common language among people who otherwise speak different languages. Russian is widely used in government and business dealings.

## TAJIK

Tajik is a language spoken by as many as 8 million people, mostly in Tajikistan, Uzbekistan, and Kyrgyzstan. Because of its close links to the main language of Iran, it was once also referred to as Farsi. In 1932, however, Joseph Stalin renamed the language "Tajik" in order to create distinctions between Persian speakers in Central Asia and Persian speakers in Iran. In 1989, Tajik was declared the state language. It is now considered separate from Farsi, at least politically. Linguists, however, still debate if it is simply a dialect of Farsi. Across the country, there are various regional dialects of Tajik. The language is also related to Dari, a similar dialect of Persian that is spoken mostly in Afghanistan. Unlike the official language of Iran, Tajik has absorbed fewer Arabic words and acquired more words from Turkic languages.

Tajik scholars believe that their language was formed mostly between the ninth and 11th centuries CE. During that time, it was written in Arabic script, and numerous fine literary works were written by authors from Bukhara, Herat, Samarqand, and other places. Scholars from present-day Tajikistan, Uzbekistan, and Iran cite these works among their countries' literary masterpieces. However, it is hard to say if they were written by native Tajik, Uzbek, or Iranian authors, since at that time there were no clear ethnic or national divisions among various Central Asian ethnic groups.

By the late 19th and early 20th centuries, Tajik had two distinctive forms: the high classical language of medieval and modern literature and poetry, with complex grammatical rules and linguistic forms; and the everyday language of the common people, which was less formal and had simplified grammatical wearing revealing outfits or little clothing or who are wearing bathing suits or underwear.

Due to the civil war and severe economic recession that followed, the population of the country has limited access to international media, since subscriptions to foreign newspapers and magazines are prohibitively expensive for most people and access to the Internet is still significantly limited in Tajikistan. On the positive side, the government has removed all restrictions on the ownership of satellite dishes, and many Tajiks now use them as a vital source of news and entertainment. Sometimes neighboring families, in order to reduce the financial burden, share a single satellite dish.

Being such a mountainous and rural nation, Tajikistan has been slow to get internet services to people far beyond the cities. In 2016, about 20.5 percent of the population was thought to have access to the internet.

The offices of Safina TV in Dushanbe are shown here. The station is one of several state television channels, offering social and analytical programs. news, and entertainment.

## INTERNET LINKS

**https://www.mustgo.com/worldlanguages/tajik**
This overview of the Tajik language includes its historical background.

**https://omniglot.com/writing/tajik.htm**
This language site provides a quick introduction to the Tajik language.

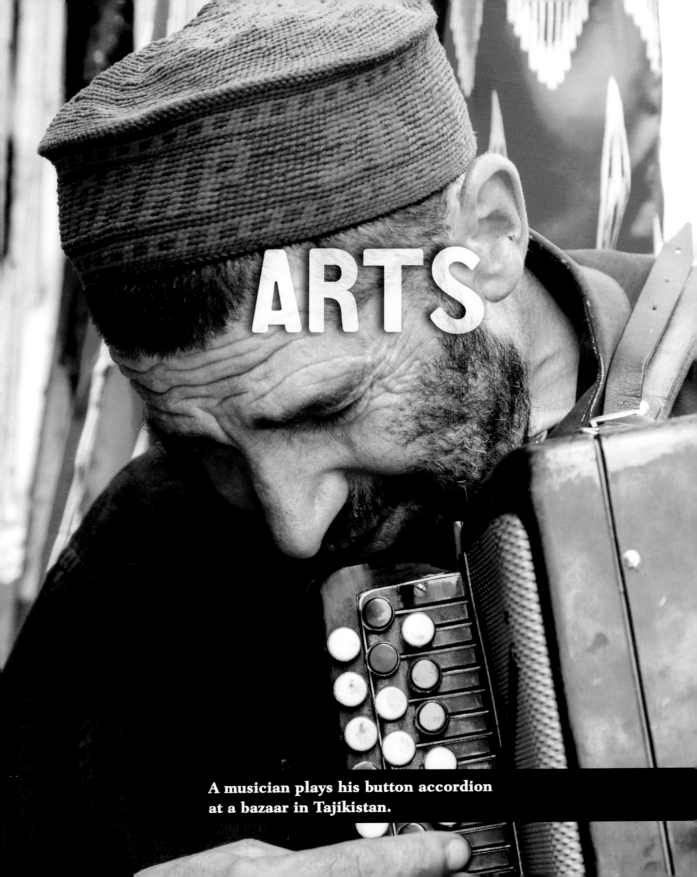

# ARTS

A musician plays his button accordion
at a bazaar in Tajikistan.

## 10

# T

HE ARTS IN TAJIKISTAN REFLECT both the country's deep past and recent history. Tajik masters are known as excellent architects, potters, and jewelry makers. Woolen rugs and silk dresses and scarves made by local women are in great demand in Central Asia and around the world.

Tajik scholars have traced the deep roots of contemporary Tajik arts to the nation's vibrant history and long-standing traditions. These experts find many similarities between Tajikistan's present-day artistic traditions and the many artifacts excavated from the sites of ancient and medieval cities both in Tajikistan and in neighboring lands.

## EARLY HISTORY

Ancient and medieval chronologists claim that the region was a "land of a thousand cities." Old manuscripts and miniature paintings indicate that, hundreds of years ago, cities and towns in the area were well-planned with numerous magnificent public buildings, palaces, and places of worship. Ancient craftspeople became masters of design, producing vivid paintings and imposing sculptures. The pictures and statues of mystical animals from that era still capture people's imaginations.

Archaeological excavations have found evidence of flourishing artistic communities in the states of Bactria and Sogdiana. These communities absorbed the highest achievements of ancient Greek, Persian, and Indian

*Shashmaqom* is an ancient genre of music native to pre-Islamic Tajikistan and Uzbekistan. Translated as "six maqoms," it refers to a series of song cycles based on a distinctive melodic mode that is quite different from the chromatic scale used in Western music. It's performed by a solo vocalist or a group of singers, accompanied by lutes, fiddles, handheld frame drums, and flutes.

cultures and developed their own styles. Archaeologists have discovered many sculptures and mosaic fragments, which reflect the influence of the classical traditions of Persian and Greek art. The remains of palaces and fortresses with Hellenic (Greek) columns, decorative and ritual sculptures, copper medallions, amphora-shaped pottery, and many other artifacts have been excavated and put on display in the Tajik Historical State Museum and in museums in Russia.

## ISLAMIC ARTS

The establishment of the Islamic caliphate stretching from Central Asia to North Africa secured peace in the region and made it safe to travel and trade in these vast areas. With greater wealth and stability, the arts flourished. Artistic communities were established through the generosity of rulers, princes, and wealthy individual patrons who sponsored writers, architects, and musicians.

Between the ninth and 12th centuries, the Central Asian region experienced a tremendous cultural flowering, and many scholars call this era the Central Asian Renaissance. The surviving historical artifacts show a great outpouring of artistic expression during that time, featuring a continuation of old styles as well as the creation of new visual and literary forms.

**ARCHITECTURE**   Many architectural monuments were produced during the golden era of Islamic culture. Local architects displayed great versatility and ingenuity in creating architectural forms using simple local materials such as brick, wood, and clay. They demonstrated great skill in designing the era's tallest buildings, which were able to withstand earthquakes and other natural disasters. They also built the largest domes without the use of modern machines and technologies. Famous architects and engineers from Central Asian cities were invited to places as far away as India and Egypt to help design and build palaces and mosques.

Another achievement was the development of the beautiful and colorful tiles and mosaics used to decorate the exterior and interior spaces of public buildings, palaces, and mosques. Sky-blue tiles covering domes and minarets were visible from miles away, and for centuries they withstood storms, fires, the hot sun, cold winds, and many other environmental influences without fading.

Today, the ruins of many buildings of the era can be found throughout the country. Archaeologists have excavated old fortified palaces in such places as Kalai-Kakhkakha, Munchak-Tepe, Urta-Kurgan, Pendzhikent, Kalai-Mug, and Kargani-Khisor. Khodja-Nakhshran and Muhammad Bashshar are mausoleums that stand as excellent examples of medieval Islamic religious architecture.

During the Soviet era, urban centers in Tajikistan and elsewhere in Central Asia were built up using Soviet-style architecture. Today, the capital city Dushanbe, which was called Stalinabad from 1929 to 1960, is tearing down those distinctively Soviet buildings—typically large, heavy, concrete structures—and replacing them with modern structures. In addition to removing old, deteriorating buildings, the move is seen as an attempt to de-Russify the city's culture and reclaim it for Tajikistanis.

The Abdulatif Sulton Madrasa in Istaravshan, also called the Kok Gumbaz ("Blue Dome") Mosque, dates to 1437. The appearance is typical of the architecture of this time in Central Asian history.

**LITERATURE**   During the Islamic golden age, many writers and poets produced works that gained wide acclaim in other parts of the world and have since become classics of Persian literature. Poems about love and human passion are still popular among the people, and many classic verses became well-liked songs.

Tajik scholars trace the roots of their literature to as early as the ninth and 10th centuries CE. They also claim that mid-ninth-century poet and musician Abu Abdallah Jafar Rudaki contributed to the development of early classic Tajik poetry by creating ceremonial odes, satirical poems, and beautiful lyrical verses called *ghazals*.

Tajiks also highly respect another wordsmith, Abu ol-Qasem Mansur (Firdawsi), whom they regard as the most influential poet of the era, not only in Central Asia but also in the Middle East and southern Asia. Firdawsi authored the monumental poem *Shahnameh* (*Book of Kings*). In poetic verse, he described the personal lives, loves, glories, and achievements of many generations of Central Asian rulers.

**CALLIGRAPHY AND MINIATURE PAINTING**  The rapidly developing literature of that time led to a significant creative offshoot in two related fields: calligraphy and miniature painting. Since there was no printing technology available during the era, all books were produced by hand. There was an entire social group of specialized workers who mastered the art of fine handwriting called calligraphy. The Arabic letters that were used in writing were transformed into beautiful patterns and elegant lines that were works of art in their own right. Such calligraphic writing could be seen not only in books but also adorning the walls of mosques, old public buildings, and homemade oriental carpets.

Miniature painting also had a long history in the region. Visual artists captured the beautiful landscapes, historic battles and events, and magnificent architectural monuments of the era. They depicted their subjects in great detail and peerless style. Often, these pictures are the only remaining evidence of past glories, since many of the area's cities, villages, and monuments have vanished or been destroyed in the wars and calamities that have gripped the region.

Islamic tradition forbids artists to draw humans and animals, as to prevent people from worshiping idols. Unable to paint large portraits or compositions of humans or animals, the Central Asian artistic masters created miniatures instead. They also adopted the use of more abstract forms, including rich colors and sometimes simple lines, in their art.

**MUSIC**  Music has always accompanied everyday life in Tajikistan, especially important celebrations. Typical Tajik musical instruments include various forms of percussion instruments (*tablak, nagora, doira, zang*, and *kairok*), trumpets (*karnai, nai*, and *surnai*), the fiddle, and the lute-like *dutor*. Musicians often accompanied armies and trade caravans. Those artists—*mavrigikhons* (male singers), *makomists* and *usto-navozanda* (male instrumentalists), and *sozandas* (female singers and dancers)—were always welcome and played before various audiences not only in the palaces of the rich and powerful but also at the chaikhanas (teahouses) and the homes of ordinary citizens.

One of the favorite forms of recreation in past eras was storytelling accompanied by various musical instruments. In medieval times, when

# INTANGIBLE CULTURAL HERITAGE

*Just as UNESCO (the United Nations Educational, Scientific and Cultural Organization) works to protect natural and cultural World Heritage sites, it also identifies examples of the "Intangible Cultural Heritage of Humanity" that need to be preserved. These include, according to the group's website, "traditions or living expressions inherited from our ancestors and passed on to our descendants, such as oral traditions, performing arts, social practices, rituals, arts, festive events, knowledge and practices concerning nature and the universe or the knowledge and skills to produce traditional crafts."*

*The Convention for the Safeguarding of the Intangible Cultural Heritage has listed four elements for Tajikistan. These include the embroidery art of chakan; shashmaqom, a classical music style in Tajikistan and Uzbekistan; the traditional meal of oshi palav and its social and cultural contexts; and the celebration of Nowruz, the Islamic New Year.*

A woman embroiders a large, decorative textile at a celebration of Nowruz.

*This traditional Tajik stringed instrument has a pear-shaped body and a long neck. The dutor resembles a two-string lute and is usually made of wood. The dutor is commonly used by a* dutorchy *(literally meaning "dutor player," similar to a national poet-singer) during various major events and family gatherings. Traditionally, a dutorchy was invited to sing the songs of heroes and to entertain during various public events.*

traders and the guards of camel and horse caravans stopped for the night, sometimes joined by their local friends and curious hosts, some of them would remain sleepless, on the lookout for bands of marauders or robbers. They kept themselves awake by listening to adventurous tales of past glories, distant travels, and beautiful love stories or *garibi* songs (songs about the difficulties of life far from home).

Unfortunately, many cities and towns of the era—along with most of their libraries, palaces, and greatest cultural achievements—were destroyed during the Mongol invasion in the 13th century and in the following centuries of instability and war. Legends and myths survived, but there are few tangible examples left of the region's glory and achievements in the arts during this time.

**HISTORICAL COLLECTIONS**   The National Museum in Dushanbe hosts one of the largest collections of ancient and medieval artifacts found in Tajikistan and its neighboring countries.

Tajik archaeologists have excavated many sites from ancient and medieval times, and their rich collections of jewelry, sculpture, and miniature paintings have been added to the museum's permanent holdings. Still, there are many parts of the past that remain unexplained, and scholars continue to argue about the fate of many ancient and medieval cities and events.

## 11

WHEN WORK IS DONE, Tajikistanis primarily spend their leisure time in simple ways, enjoying the company of family, friends, and neighbors. In rural areas, most events are organized around the seasons—people celebrate the beginning of spring, the end of the harvest, and other important annual milestones. In large urban areas, people enjoy leisure and entertainment activities similar to those of residents in most metropolitan areas, such as eating out and attending sports events, the theater, and parades.

In both small villages and large cities, people tend to socialize with their families or relatives and close members of their communities. Some leisure activities draw on existing religious and national traditions going back hundreds of years. Others, such as interacting with electronic media for those who have access, are signs of the times.

The Pamir Highway, M41, extends from Afghanistan though Uzbekistan and Tajikistan, ending in Osh, Kyrgyzstan. Most of the road is in Tajikistan, where it traverses the difficult mountainous terrain. Said to be the second-highest international highway in the world, it is mostly paved but is often damaged by earthquakes, landslides, and avalanches.

## FAMILY CELEBRATIONS

Important personal and family events, such as marriages, the birth of a first child or grandchild, or the building of a new home, are occasions for festive gatherings. These events are likely to be quite large. It is common to have 100 or even 200 people attending a celebration that might last anywhere from one to three days. People usually invite all their close and distant relatives, neighbors, colleagues, and friends.

The celebrations are organized in a grand manner, with music, dance, and plenty of food and drink. Such events need to be planned well in advance, and many people are involved in the organizational process. It is also expected that the guests will help with such events either by contributing small sums of money or lending furniture, providing transportation or food for the event, or just helping to set up and clean afterward.

These gatherings are more than simple family celebrations. They serve as excellent occasions for networking as well. They are opportunities to learn about the developments and achievements in the personal lives of friends and colleagues. These celebrations are also regularly used by young people to meet potential partners or by their parents for matchmaking. For young artists and musicians, these events serve as ideal opportunities to show off their talents and gain greater recognition and followings.

For Westerners, it might seem unusual to invite a stranger to a family event, but that is not the case in Tajikistan. Whoever happens to be in the neighborhood is invited to join the fun, including foreigners. Even former rivals come to the gatherings, since they provide an excellent opportunity for reconciliation.

## GAPS

In traditional Tajik society, people organize themselves into informal interest groups called *gaps* (meaning "talk" or "discussion"). A gap is a group of friends or neighbors who get together for entertainment or the discussion of various political or nonpolitical issues. Such gatherings help provide mutual support the past. In an informal and captivating way, they extract moral and personal lessons for their young listeners, whom they hope will make the tales and the art of storytelling part of their own family traditions.

In chaikhanas, storytelling is a part of the general entertainment. A skillful storyteller will recount stories about the life and adventures of one of the nation's favorite comic personalities—Afandi. Local heroes or the colorful figures of the past and present are also the subjects of these vivid tales.

Sometimes, friends and colleagues come together to listen to and discuss stories taken from the pages of Tajik history, literature, and poetry. Others focus on tales about Islamic characters. Those gathered often invite local musicians, singers, or poets to present their creative works or to relate favorite legends in the form of songs.

## INTERNET LINKS

**https://www.forbes.com/sites/willnicoll/2020/04/30/ tajikistan-soccer-and-the-dictatorships-profiting-from-covid- 19/#181a9420d034**
This article alleges corrupt connections between Tajikistan's rulers and its pro soccer league.

**https://www.unesco-ichcap.org/kor/ek/sub2017_6/pdf_down/7. percent20TRADITIONAL percent20SPORT percent20AND percent20CHILDREN percent20GAMES/1. percent20Wrestling.pdf**
This pdf published by UNESCO provides some information and photos about Tajik traditional wrestling.

**https://us.soccerway.com/teams/tajikistan/tajikistan/2205**
This is an entry for Tajikistan's national football team on a U.S. soccer site.

# FESTIVALS

Women in colorful national costumes celebrate the 25th anniversary of Tajikistan's independence on September 9, 2016, at Dusti (Friendship) Square in Dushanbe.

# 12

FESTIVE OCCASIONS IN TAJIKISTAN are mostly secular, historic, and patriotic events, but the two most important Muslim holidays are also observed. These are annual public holidays, in which workers and students typically have a day off. In addition, some regional arts, food, and sporting events take place, but they are relatively few compared with those of many other countries.

During the years of Soviet control, religious holidays, such as Nowruz and the Muslim holy days, were forbidden. Since independence in 1991, though, Islamic observances have been firmly reestablished in Tajik life, and the largely secular Nowruz is also enthusiastically embraced. Only one of the old Soviet patriotic days remains on the Tajik calendar: Victory Day on May 9, which commemorates the end of World War II and the victory of the Allies (the United States, Great Britain, the Soviet Union, France, and others), against the Axis nations (Nazi Germany, Italy, and Japan).

## NOWRUZ

Nowruz, or Navruz, is a spring festival that has been celebrated by Tajikistanis since pre-Islamic times. In fact, the ancient holiday is marked throughout central and south Asia, Iran, and Turkey. The roots of the holiday reach back to the region's Zoroastrian heritage, and the important

Sayri Guli Lola is a tulip festival in Tajikistan. This festival is celebrated with flower and garden competitions and songs and dancing across the country. Tulips are native to the region and were the source for the famous Dutch tulips. In 2020, almost 5 million tulips were planted in Dushanbe to mark the 30th anniversary of the republic.

A young woman carries a dish of grass sprouts, a traditional symbol of spring, to a celebration of Nowruz. The holiday marks the beginning of spring.

Zoroastrian element of fire figures in the celebrations—leaping over a bonfire is one of the holiday's main traditions.

Nowruz goes by many variations of its name, but they all mean "new day." People often call it the Spring Festival because it starts on the first day of spring—the spring equinox, usually March 21—according to the solar calendar. Nowruz was not celebrated during Tajikistan's Soviet era, but it was reintroduced as a national holiday after 1991.

One of the nation's most beloved festivals, Nowruz is traditionally celebrated in a grand way. Local communities and governments usually organize performances of various musical and dance groups in their town or city's major public parks or central squares. Merchants set up outdoor food stands and large bazaars. Families typically visit one another or attend major community events. The festival is also an opportunity for everyone to watch performances by local artists or to take part in them.

## HOLIDAYS AND OBSERVANCES IN TAJIKISTAN

*January 1 . . . . . . . New Year's Day*
*March 8 . . . . . . . International Women's Day*
*March 21–24 . . . . . Nowruz Celebration (spring holiday)*
*May 9 . . . . . . . . Victory Day (surrender of Nazi Germany in World War II)*
*June 27 . . . . . . . . Day of National Unity (civil war peace treaty of 1997)*
*September 9 . . . . . Independence Day (primary national holiday)*
*November 6 . . . . . Constitution Day (adoption of constitution in 1996)*
*Islamic holidays (changeable dates):*
*Eid al-Fitr*
*Eid Kurban*

Many Tajikistanis believe that Nowruz unleashes good will and good luck that extends throughout the entire year. It is a special time of renewal when people tend to buy new clothes and make gifts for one another.

In 2016, UNESCO added Nowruz to its List of Intangible Cultural Heritage of Humanity, listing Tajikistan as one of its 12 representative nations.

## ISLAMIC FESTIVALS

Muslim festivals are celebrated according to the Islamic lunar calendar. The lunar year is 10 or 11 days shorter than the Gregorian calendar year used in most Western countries. Therefore, all events and festivals in the lunar calendar are moved forward 10 or 11 days every year.

**RAMADAN** Ramadan is the ninth month in the Islamic calendar, when all devoted Muslims are encouraged to fast from sunrise to sunset. Fasting is one of the Five Pillars of Islam and is considered to be an important duty for every Muslim.

According to Islamic teaching, it was during Ramadan that the Prophet Muhammad began receiving messages from God. Fasting during Ramadan reminds people of the difficulties faced by the poor, teaches self-discipline, and helps them cleanse themselves of selfishness and open their hearts to the teachings of God. It is expected that all Muslims refrain from any wrongdoing, harming of others, or fighting with one another during the month. Islamic doctrine does allow for some exceptions. For example, pregnant or nursing women, travelers, or the sick are allowed to abstain from fasting during Ramadan. However, they are required to fast for the same number of days they missed later in the year.

As most Muslims fast during Ramadan, some restaurants, cafés, teahouses and food stores in Tajikistan are closed during the daytime and open in the evening. However, the nation is not as strict as other Muslim countries, particularly those in the Middle East. Many shops and food stores in Tajikistan remain open during Ramadan since there are communities of non-Muslims. Still, business and public work tend to slow down during this time.

People break their fasts after sunset. It is always done in a grand way, as many family members, friends, colleagues, and neighbors come together to share a prayer and then food. Children use this opportunity to visit other houses, where they receive small gifts from adults, usually in the form of candy and sweets. Rich and successful people are strongly encouraged to invite poor members of the community to their homes to share food after sunset.

**EID AL-FITR**    This is one of the two most important holidays in the Islamic calendar. It signifies the end of the fasting that comes with the observance of Ramadan. Muslims celebrate Eid al-Fitr together and use this time to visit, since it is strongly encouraged that doors be opened to all members of the community and that everyone visit one another without special invitation. Traditionally, wealthy members of the community are expected to organize major feasts and to invite their relatives and neighbors to share their good fortune and success.

**EID KURBAN**    Known as Eid al-Adha in the Arab world, Eid Kurban is the Feast of the Sacrifice. It commemorates the biblical sacrifice of Abraham (Ibrahim), in which God (Allah) ordered him to kill his son as a show of obedience. As Ibrahim prepared to obey, Allah, at the last second, spared the child. This most holy of Islamic holidays takes place in the 12th month of the lunar calendar, when Muslims commemorate the end of a hajj, a pilgrimage to the holy city of Mecca. As with all other Islamic festivals, the date that the holiday is observed shifts each calendar year. The day is an opportunity to recognize all members of the family, to visit the graves of relatives, and to give food to the poor.

Traditionally, families buy a whole lamb (the animal sacrificed in place of Ibrahim's son) for this festival and organize a big feast for their extended family and close friends. People are also encouraged to make donations to various charities or to poor members of their communities.

## FAMILY FEASTS

Many people in Tajikistan have a strong sense of family, and they use every possible opportunity to meet with close and distant relatives and to bring extended families together. There is even an informal rule that all family members should take turns organizing feasts at their homes during the year, so a large extended family visits each of its members' homes at least once or twice a year. People believe that this helps keep strong ties among the various family members and allows them to provide the necessary support to one another in times of need or congratulations and best wishes in times of success.

## INTERNET LINKS

**https://ich.unesco.org/en/RL/nawrouz-novruz-nowrouz-nowrouz-nawrouz-nauryz-nooruz-nowruz-navruz-nevruz-nowruz-navruz-01161**
This page is the Intangible Heritage listing for Nowruz.

**https://www.timeanddate.com/holidays/tajikistan**
This calendar site lists public holidays yearly.

# FOOD

A vendor offers prepared foods at the
Panjshanbe Bazaar in Khujand.

## 13

THE CUISINE OF CENTRAL ASIA IS quite similar across its five countries. This makes sense, as the countries' culture and history have much in common. The typical meals tend to include lamb, rice, some vegetables, flatbreads, and tea; they reflect ancient Persian influences and the traditional lifestyle of nomadic, rural peoples. In the 19th and 20th centuries, Russia exerted its rule over the region, adding Russian cooking styles to the mix.

Being a majority Muslim people, Tajikistanis and their Central Asian neighbors do not eat pork because it is not permitted by Islamic tradition. They prefer lamb, chicken, goat, and some beef. In contrast to their neighbors to the northeast in Kyrgyzstan, however, Tajikistanis don't eat horse meat. Also, as Tajikistan is a landlocked country, seafood plays little role in the usual menu.

For all the region's shared food culture, however, there are regional variations across Central Asia and even within Tajikistan itself. The cuisine of the Pamir Mountains, for example, can be quite different from the dishes popular in metropolitan Dushanbe or northern Tajikistan. The ubiquitous rice pilaf, for example, called *plov* or *osh*, has countless subtle variations from city to city and town to town.

Traditionally, Tajikistanis have a strong sense of hospitality. It is customary to invite a guest or even a visiting stranger to share food

Although international hotels in the cities serve Western-style breakfasts, the average Tajikistani is more likely to start the day with bread and tea. If the family can afford it, jam and butter might be served with the bread. Kefir, a yogurt-like drink, is also often served with breakfast.

Women sell *non* (flatbread) at a bazaar in Khujand.

with one's family. These meals can take several hours at lunch and especially at dinner, since people often discuss family affairs, current events, or even business deals over elaborate meals. Hosts usually offer several courses and large quantities of food. They would be offended if their guests did not eat or ate only a little.

## A TYPICAL MEAL

Meals often start with a cup of green tea or a piece of homemade flatbread called *non* (sometimes referred to as the Russian *lipioshka*). This is followed by soup, usually made of meat and various vegetables and perhaps homemade noodles. After the soup comes the main dish. Often the principal course is a rice pilaf dish of meat, onions, and thinly cut carrots or turnips. Some cooks add herbs, apricots, raisins, garlic, nuts, quinces, or any number of other ingredients to plov. The meal usually ends with fresh fruit in the form of apples, pears, grapes, watermelons, honeydew melons, or fresh or dried apricots. In addition, guests are always served plenty of tea.

## OTHER POPULAR FOODS

Favorite dishes include *shashkyl* (kebabs), *manti* (steamed dumplings stuffed with meat, often served with minted sour cream), *laghman* (Chinese-style noodles with meat and vegetables), and various meat and vegetable soups. Salads of chopped tomato, onion, and cucumbers are a common side dish. Street food includes *sambusas* (or *samsas*), which are savory baked pastries filled with onions and chopped meat or pumpkin.

One dish that is exclusive to Tajikistan is *qurutob*, which is often called the national dish. This recipe calls for soaking flatbread in a salty, yogurt-like

Grilled lamb kebabs, served with sliced raw onions and tomatoes and a loaf of non in a basket, is a typical meal in Tajikistan.

A woman stokes a fire in a large tandoor oven to bake flatbreads, in a kishlak (rural settlement) in Sughd Province.

cheese, and topping it with onions and other vegetables. The qurutob is served on one large platter for communal dining and eaten with one's hand.

Dairy products are typically made from the milk of sheep, cows, goats, horses, and camels. These include cheeses; yogurt; cottage cheese; *aryan,* a yogurt drink; *chaka,* a kind of sour milk; *qurut,* dried salted cheese balls that form the base of qurutob; and *kaymak,* a sweet clotted cream.

Bread is served at every meal and comes in many forms of flatbread. These are often baked in a special round brick, clay, or metal oven called a tandoor, which is usually fired with charcoal or wood. Raw dough rounds are stuck to the hot oven walls, where they cook very quickly. Although some cooks will bake bread at home, loaves of flatbread are easily found at food markets.

## DINING TRADITIONS

Meals are almost always prepared at home, with young children helping their parents, learning cooking skills from an early age. Often, in order to show

# "THE KING OF MEALS"

*One of the four elements for Tajikistan inscribed on the UNESCO List of Intangible Cultural Heritage is based on its food culture. The plov, osh, or pilaf dish that the organization calls* oshi palav *was added to the list in 2016. This traditional Tajik dish, known as the "king of meals," is served at everyday meals, as well as at social gatherings, celebrations, and rituals. The organization reports that around 200 varieties of the dish exist across Tajikistan, and it's considered so integral a part of the culture that it is part of local sayings such as "No osh, no acquaintance" (meaning you don't know someone until you have*

Cooks dish up servings of a huge pot of plov as part of the Oshi Palav Festival in Dushanbe.

*eaten osh with them) or "If you have eaten osh [prepared by or offered by] someone, you must respect them for 40 years."*

*Just as eating the pilaf is a social experience, so, too, is preparing it. Groups of men or women will make the dish at home or at teahouses while chatting, playing music, or singing.*

particular respect to especially honored guests, male members of the family cook the meal themselves, though everyday food is traditionally cooked by the female members of the families.

Cooperation among family members is particularly important, because in many parts of Tajikistan, modern kitchen appliances and facilities are uncommon. In many villages and small towns, people use natural gas or, if gas is not available, wood or coal.

Meals are eaten around a low table—or a tablecloth spread on the floor—called a *dastarkhan*. Food is served communally and often eaten by hand or dished into soup bowls or small plates for salads. Customarily, the family will wait to eat until the most senior person takes a bite.

## DRINKS AND SWEETS

Traditionally, Tajikistanis do not drink carbonated beverages or fruit juices, though in recent years the younger generations have increasingly embraced these kinds of drinks. Otherwise, the single most important and most popular drink is tea.

People often prefer green tea because they believe that green tea is the best drink to overcome not only thirst but dehydration. Black, herbal, and fruit teas are also popular in more rural areas.

Local people drink tea in a rural area of Tajikistan.

Tajikistanis serve teas with various dried fruits, including apricots, raisins, dried honeydew melons, and berries. In many parts of the country, people also add various nuts to their tea, including walnuts, pistachios, and almonds. Coffee and hot chocolate are the chosen drinks of sophisticated urbanites, but they are almost unseen in the rural areas.

Alcohol is served during some celebrations, although the practice of Islam generally forbids its consumption. Locally made vodkas and sweet wines, along with various imported brandies and other strong liquors, can be found in all major stores and restaurants.

Dessert is not generally thought of as an after-dinner course. Rather, sweet dishes are served alongside the meal or with tea afterward. Fresh or dried fruit is most typical, but Tajikistanis might also serve halvah (a sweet dessert typically made of nuts), or homemade bread and cookies topped with various homemade jams. In urban areas, ice cream has become an increasingly popular treat.

## TEA RITUALS

For centuries, Central Asians have mastered the fine art of serving and consuming tea, developing complex rituals along the way. Table etiquette is very important in Tajikistan, since local tradition, social status, age, position in the family hierarchy, and many other factors are taken into consideration when serving tea.

People usually drink green tea served in small teapots. It is customary for the youngest person at the table to serve the others assembled. Alternatively, the host serves tea herself or himself in order to show great respect to the guests. Local etiquette often requires that all food and drink be received with the right hand. Traditionally, when the tea has been freshly made, people pour some into a teacup, return it to the teapot, and then repeat this twice to facilitate the brewing process. Certain positions around the table are reserved for the most respected person, usually an aksakal, who starts and ends the meal and generally leads the conversation.

## INTERNET LINKS

**https://www.advantour.com/tajikistan/cuisine.htm**
This travel site offers a look at the cuisine of Tajikistan.

**https://www.dookinternational.com/blog/most-popular-Central-asian-cuisines-and-food/**
Photos of popular Central Asian foods include some Tajik specialties.

**http://factsanddetails.com/Central-asia/Tajikistan/sub8_6b/entry-4878.html**
This reference site lists information about food and drinks in Tajikistan.

# *PLOV* (TAJIK RICE PILAF)

½ cup (120 mililiters) vegetable oil

2 pounds (about 1 kilogram) of lamb,
   cubed into bite-sized pieces

2 onions, peeled, halved, and thinly sliced

7 to 8 carrots, peeled and cut in long,
   thin sticks

1 tablespoon cumin

4 cups hot water

2 cups (380 grams) of uncooked white rice
   (preferably basmati)

½ cup raisins and/or 10 dried apricots,
   chopped (optional)

1 whole head of garlic

salt to taste

Heat the oil over high heat in a large pan. Brown the lamb on all sides. Turn the heat to medium, and add the onions and carrots. Cook until soft, and stir in the cumin and salt. Add enough water to cover the meat and carrots. Cover, and simmer for 35 to 40 minutes on medium heat.

Meanwhile, rinse the rice in cold water 2 or 3 times. After the meat has cooked, add the rice to the pan. Add the hot water and salt, making sure the rice is submerged. Simmer 15 minutes uncovered, then add the dried fruit if using. Place the head of garlic in the center of the rice. Cover, and steam another 15 to 20 minutes.

Serves 5—6.

## *SHAKAROB* (TOMATO ONION SALAD)

2 onions (red or white), thinly sliced
6 ripe tomatoes, cut into wedges
salt and pepper to taste
cilantro or basil, chopped fresh
pomegranate seeds (optional)

Soak the sliced onions in salted cold water (enough to cover) for at least 10 minutes. Drain well. Place in serving bowl with tomatoes, season with salt and pepper, and sprinkle with cilantro or basil. Add pomegranate seeds to taste. This salad is served without dressing.

# MAP OF TAJIKISTAN

F

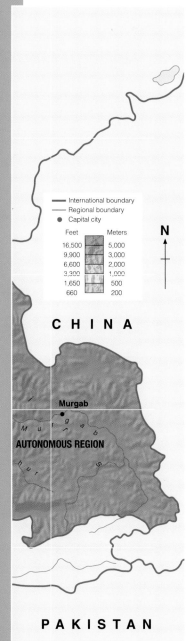

International boundary
Regional boundary
● Capital city

| Feet | Meters |
|---|---|
| 16,500 | 5,000 |
| 9,900 | 3,000 |
| 6,600 | 2,000 |
| 3,300 | 1,000 |
| 1,650 | 500 |
| 660 | 200 |

N

C H I N A

AUTONOMOUS REGION

P A K I S T A N

Afghanistan, A5,
   B4—B5, C3—C5,
   D5, E4—E5,
   F4—F5
Alai Range, C2—C3,
   D2, E2
Alichur (river),
   D4—F4
Amu Darya (river),
   A5, B4—B5

Bokhtar, B4

China, E2—E3,
   F1—F5

Dushanbe, B3

Fergana Valley,
   B2—C2

Gorno-Badakhshan
   Autonomous
   Region, C3—C4,
   D2—D5, E2—E5,
   F3—F4

Hisor, A3

Ismail Samani, D3

Karl Marx Peak,
   D5—E5
Khatlon, A3—A5,
   B3—B5, C3—C4
Khorugh, D4
Khujand, B2
Kofamihon (river),
   A3—A5, B3
Kuli Sarez, E3—E4
Kulob, B4
Kyrgyzstan, B2, C2,
   D1—D2, E1—E2,
   F1—F2

Langar, B2

Murgab, F4
Murgab (river),
   E3—E4, F4

Nurek, B3

Obanbori
   Qayroqqum, B2,
   C1—C2

Pakistan, D5—F5
Pamirs, D3, E3—E4,
   F3—F4
Panj (river), D5—F5
Pendzhikent, A2

Qarokul, E3

Ramit, B3
Revolyutsiya, D3

Sirdar'inskiy, B2
Sughd Province,
   A2—A3, B1—B3,
   C1—C2
Surkhob (river),
   B3—C3
Syr Darya (river),
   C1—D1

Tursunzade, A3

Uzbekistan, A1—A4,
   B1—B2, C1—C2,
   D1—D2, E1

Vakhsh (river),
   A4—A5, B3—B4

Yashilkul, E4

Zeravshan (river),
   A2

# ECONOMIC TAJIKISTAN

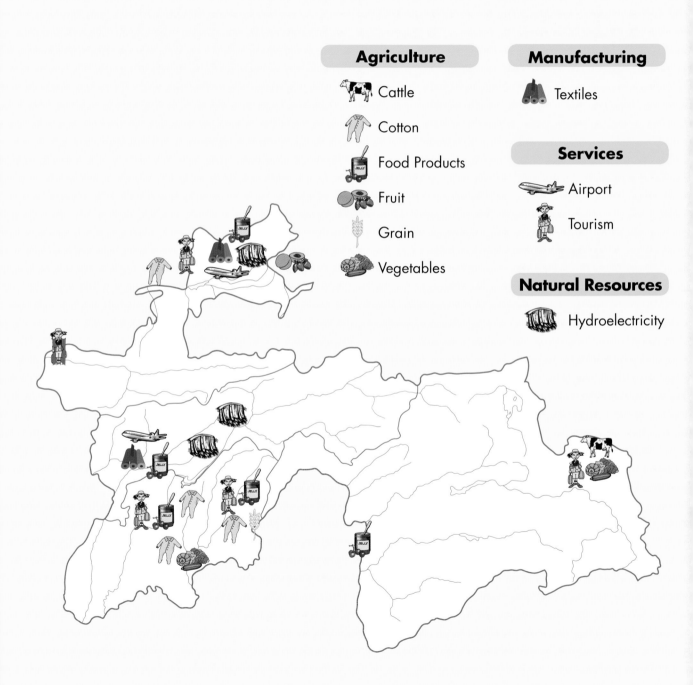

# ABOUT THE ECONOMY

*All figures are 2017 estimates unless otherwise noted.*

## GROSS DOMESTIC PRODUCT (OFFICIAL EXCHANGE RATE)
$7.144 billion

## GDP PER CAPITA
$3,200

## GDP BY SECTOR
agriculture: 28.6 percent
industry: 25.5 percent
services: 45.9 percent

## WORKFORCE
2.3 million (2016)

## WORKFORCE BY OCCUPATION
agriculture: 43 percent
industry: 10.6 percent
services: 46.4 percent (2016)

## CURRENCY
Tajikistani somoni (TJS) = 100 diram
notes: 1, 5, 20, 50 diram; 20, 50, 100, 200, 500 somoni
coins: 1, 5, 10, 20, 25, 50 diram; 1, 3, 5 somoni
$1 USD = 10.33 Tajikistani somoni (July 2020)

## POPULATION BELOW POVERTY LINE
31.5 percent (2016)

## AGRICULTURAL PRODUCTS
cotton, grain, fruits, grapes, vegetables, cattle, sheep, goats

## INDUSTRIAL PRODUCTS
aluminum, cement, coal, gold, silver, antimony

## MAIN EXPORTS
aluminum, electricity, cotton, fruits, vegetable oil, textiles

## MAIN IMPORTS
petroleum products, aluminum oxide, machinery and equipment, food

## TRADE PARTNERS
Russia, Kazakhstan, Turkey, China, Iran

# CULTURAL TAJIKISTAN

**Rudaki Museum**
This museum named after the ninth-century poet Abu Abdallah Jafar Rudaki preserves artifacts from the ancient city of Penjikent. Excavations have also uncovered the ruins of homes and Zoroastrian temples in Penjikent.

**Petroglyphs**
Rock carvings in caves above the town of Langar depict caravans and men riding horses.

**Historical and Cultural Reserve**
Hisor is home to the ruins of Hisor Fort and the 16th-century Sangin Mosque and Makhdumi Azam mausoleum.

**National Museum of Tajikistan**
This museum in Dushanbe features ancient Greek, Bactrian, and Persian sculptures, paintings, and jewelry.

**Ajina-Tepe**
This ancient Buddhist monastery, 7.5 miles (12 km) northeast of Bokhtar, includes a 39-foot (12 m) Buddha statue.

**Mir Said Khamadoni Mausoleum**
Kulob hosts the mausoleum of the great poet Mir Said Khamadoni.

# ABOUT THE CULTURE

*All figures are 2020 estimates unless otherwise noted.*

**OFFICIAL NAME**
Republic of Tajikistan

**POPULATION**
8,873,670

**ETHNIC GROUPS**
Tajik 84.3 percent (includes Pamiri and Yagnobi), Uzbek 13.8 percent, other 2 percent (includes Kyrgyz, Russian, Turkmen, Tatar, Arab) (2014)

**RELIGIOUS GROUPS**
Muslim 98 percent (Sunni 95 percent, Shia 3 percent), other 2 percent (2014)

**LANGUAGES**
Tajik (official) 84.4 percent, Uzbek 11.9 percent, Kyrgyz 0.8 percent, Russian 0.5 percent, other 2.4 percent (2010)
*Note:* Russian widely used in government and business

**POPULATION GROWTH RATE**
1.52 percent

**URBANIZATION**
27.5 percent of total population

**MAJOR URBAN AREA**
Dushanbe (capital), population 916,000

**INFANT MORTALITY RATE**
28.8 deaths per 1,000 live births

**LIFE EXPECTANCY AT BIRTH**
total population: 69 years
male: 65.9 years
female: 72.3 years

**LITERACY RATE**
99.8 percent (2015)

# TIMELINE

| IN TAJIKISTAN | IN THE WORLD |
|---|---|
| **Second century BCE** | |
| The Great Silk Road starts to function. | **117 CE** |
| | The Roman Empire reaches its greatest extent. |
| **Seventh to eighth centuries CE** | **CE 600** |
| Arabs conquer Central Asia. | The height of the Maya civilization is reached. |
| | **1000** |
| **1221–1222** | The Chinese perfect gunpowder and |
| Genghis Khan conquers Central Asia. | begin to use it in warfare. |
| **1384** | |
| Timur invades Khorasan. | **1530** |
| | The transatlantic slave trade begins. |
| | **1620** |
| | The Pilgrims sail to America. |
| | **1776** |
| | The U.S. Declaration of Independence is written. |
| | **1789–1799** |
| **1826–1828** | The French Revolution takes place. |
| The Russian-Persian War is fought. | **1861–1865** |
| | The American Civil War takes place. |
| | **1869** |
| **1887** | The Suez Canal opens. |
| The borders of Russia's possessions in | |
| Central Asia are formally established. | **1914–1918** |
| **1922** | World War I is fought. |
| Union of Soviet Socialist Republics | |
| (USSR) is established. | |
| **1924** | |
| The Tajik Autonomous Soviet | |
| Socialist Republic is established. | |
| **1929–1938** | |
| Mass collectivization programs begin; | |
| mass purges against Tajik intelligentsia | |
| and political leadership take place. | |
| **1937** | |
| The constitution of the Tajik SSR is adopted. | **1939–1945** |
| | World War II devastates Europe. |
| | **1966–1969** |
| | The Chinese Cultural Revolution takes place. |

| IN TAJIKISTAN | IN THE WORLD |
|---|---|
| | **• 1969** |
| | U.S. astronaut Neil Armstrong becomes |
| **1978 •** | the first human on the moon. |
| The Tajik SSR adopts a new constitution. | |
| | |
| **1991 •** | **• 1991** |
| Tajikistan declares independence. | The Soviet Union breaks up. |
| **1992 •** | |
| Emomali Rahmonov becomes | |
| president of Tajikistan. | |
| **1992–1997 •** | **• 1997** |
| A civil war is fought in Tajikistan. | Britain returns Hong Kong to China. |
| | **• 2001** |
| | Terrorists attack the United States on September 11. |
| | |
| **2004 •** | |
| The Tajik parliament outlaws the death penalty. | |
| **2006 •** | |
| Rahmonov wins a third term, but international | |
| observers say the election is neither free nor fair. | |
| **2007 •** | |
| President Rahmonov bans Russian- | **• 2008** |
| style surnames for newborns, and drops the | Americans elect their first African |
| Russian ending -ov from his own name. | American president, Barack Obama. |
| **2015 •** | **• 2015–2016** |
| The government bans the leading opposition | ISIS launches terror attacks in Belgium and France. |
| party, the Islamic Renaissance Party of Tajikistan. | |
| **2016 •** | |
| Work begins on the Rogun hydroelectric dam. | |
| **2017 •** | **• 2017** |
| Rahmon takes new title as Leader of the Nation. | Donald Trump becomes U.S. president. |
| | Hurricanes devastate Caribbean islands. |
| **2018 •** | **• 2018** |
| Four international tourists are | The Winter Olympics are held in South Korea. |
| killed in a terror attack. | **• 2019** |
| | Notre Dame Cathedral in Paris is damaged by fire. |
| **2020 •** | **• 2020** |
| Tajik Football League play is suspended | The COVID-19 pandemic spreads across the world. |
| indefinitely due to the COVID-19 pandemic. | |

# GLOSSARY

**aksakal**
An elder; a respected older member of a local community.

**chaikhana**
A traditional teahouse in Central Asia.

**gap**
An informal interest group in traditional Tajik society. Members may be friends or neighbors, and topics range from personal to professional.

**Ismailis**
An Islamic sect with close links to the teachings of Shia Islam.

**kalym**
A payment in the form of money or gifts that is expected to be paid by the family of a bridegroom to the family of a bride.

**kishlak**
A rural settlement in Tajikistan.

**madrassa**
An Islamic religious school.

**mahallya**
A neighborhood community in Tajikistan and other parts of Central Asia.

**mullah**
An Islamic scholar.

**Nowruz**
A spring festival in Tajikistan and other parts of Central Asia.

**Ramadan**
The ninth month in the Islamic calendar; a time for fasting and the atonement of sins.

**Zoroastrianism**
An ancient religion originating in Central Asia.

# FOR FURTHER INFORMATION

## BOOKS

Fatland, Erka. *Sovietistan: A Journey Through Turkmenistan, Kazakhstan, Tajikistan, Kyrgyzstan and Uzbekistan.* London, UK: MacLehose Press/Hachette, 2019.

Gillmore, Ged, and Bernadette Kearns. *Stans By Me: A Whirlwind Tour Through Central Asia.* Paddington, New South Wales, Australia: de Grevilo Publishing, 2019.

Ibbotson, Sophie, and Max Lovell-Hoare. *Tajikistan*. Chalfont St. Peter, UK: Bradt Travel Guides, 2018.

Lioy, Stephen, and Anna Kamininski et al., *Lonely Planet Central Asia*, 7th edition. Franklin, TN: Lonely Planet Publishing, 2018.

## ONLINE

BBC News. "Tajikistan Country Profile." https://www.bbc.com/news/world-asia-16201032.

CIA. *The World Factbook*. "Tajikistan." https://www.cia.gov/library/publications/the-world-factbook/geos/ti.html.

*Encylopaedia Britannica*. "Tajikistan." https://www.britannica.com/place/Tajikistan.

Eurasianet. "Tajikistan." https://eurasianet.org/region/tajikistan.

National Information Agency of Tajikistan. https://eng.khovar.tj.

## FILMS

*Emergency in Tajikistan*. Piggery Productions/Ananda Media, 2014.

*The Silence*. Arrow Films, 1998.

## MUSIC

*Folk Music of Tajikistan*, I—IV. Mehrnigori Rustam. World Music, 2020.

*Tajikistan: Classical Music & Songs*. Abduvali Abdurashidov/Outhere, 2013.

# BIBLIOGRAPHY

BBC News. "Tajikistan Country Profile." https://www.bbc.com/news/world-asia-16201032.

BBC News. "Timeline." https://www.bbc.com/news/world-asia-16201087.

CIA. *The World Factbook*. "Tajikistan." https://www.cia.gov/library/publications/the-world-factbook/geos/ti.html.

*Encyclopaedia Britannica*. "Tajikistan." https://www.britannica.com/place/Tajikistan.

Radio Free Europe/Radio Liberty. "Last Survivor of Group That Killed Foreign Cyclists in Tajikistan Dies in Prison." March 3, 2020. https://www.rferl.org/a/last-survivor-of-group-that-killed-foreign-cyclists-in-tajikistan-dies-in-prison/30465829.html.

UNECE. "Tajikistan Environmental Performance Reviews, Third Review." United Nations Economic Commission for Europe, 2017. https://www.unece.org/fileadmin/DAM/env/epr/epr_studies/ECE.CEP.180.Eng.pdf.

UNESCO Intangible Cultural Heritage. "Tajikistan." https://ich.unesco.org/en/state/tajikistan-TJ.

UNESCO World Heritage. "Tajikistan." https://whc.unesco.org/en/statesparties/tj.

World Bank. "Tajikistan Overview." https://www.worldbank.org/en/country/tajikistan/overview.

# INDEX

# INDEX